OUT

OF
THE
DEPTHS

Also by Cathy MacPhail

Run, Zan, Run
Missing
Bad Company
Dark Waters
Fighting Back
Another Me
Underworld
Roxy's Baby
Worse Than Boys
Grass

The Nemesis Series
Into the Shadows
The Beast Within
Sinister Intent
Ride of Death

OUT OF THE DEPTHS

CATHY MACPHAIL

BLOOMSBURY

LONDON NEW DELHI NEW YORK SYDNEY

Acknowledgements
A book is inspired by so many different things.
I was asked by Tynecastle High School in Edinburgh
to supply them with a first line for a story competition,
and they challenged me to write a story using that same first
line. Hadn't a clue what I was going to write. Until I visited
another school, St Joseph's College in Dumfries, and the
pupils there were so keen for me to use their wonderfully
atmospheric school in a book. And then, in another
school, I met the real Tyler Lawless, and it all came
together. Light-bulb moment.
Thank you all.

Bloomsbury Publishing, London, New Delhi, New York and Sydney

First published in Great Britain in November 2011
by Bloomsbury Publishing Plc
50 Bedford Square, London, WC1B 3DP

A CIP catalogue record for this book is available from the British Library

ISBN 978 0 7475 9909 8

MIX
Paper from
responsible sources
FSC
www.fsc.org   FSC® C020471

Typeset by Dorchester Typesetting Group Ltd
Printed and bound in Great Britain
by CPI Group (UK), Croydon CR0 4YY

3 5 7 9 10 8 6 4

www.bloomsbury.com
www.cathymacphail.com

For a Beloved Sister,
Teresa

I saw my teacher in the queue at the supermarket last Christmas. Miss Baxter. I was surprised to see her. She'd been dead for six months.

She saw me. I know she saw me. In fact, I could swear her eyes were searching me out. As if she was watching for me.

As if she'd been waiting for me.

I hurried towards her, pushing people aside, but you know what it's like at Christmas. Queues at all the checkouts, crowds with trolleys piled high with shopping, everything and everyone blocking your way. By the time I got to where I'd seen her, she was gone. No sign of her anywhere.

And when I told them at school no one would believe me. 'Typical Tyler Lawless,' they all said. 'You're always making up stories.'

Even my best friend, Annabelle, agreed with them. She'd sounded annoyed at me. Wanted me to be just an ordinary, run-of-the-mill best friend who didn't cause her any embarrassment.

I had let my imagination run away with me, everyone said. It was just another of my stories. It's true I want to be a writer, and I do look for stories everywhere. You're supposed to do that. But this time I wasn't making it up. I really did see her.

Miss Baxter had died abroad during the summer holidays. A tragic accident, they said. An accident that should never have happened. Her body had been brought back and she was buried somewhere in England.

But I had seen her!

I couldn't stop thinking about her. Trying to find an explanation for the unexplainable. And I began to think . . . what if she hadn't died at all? What if someone else's body had been identified as hers? What if it was all a scam to get the life insurance?

Or what if she was in the witness protection programme and had had to change her identity?

'She'd hardly be likely to pop into the local supermarket then, would she?' Annabelle scoffed at me. And if she couldn't believe me, what chance did I have with anyone else?

I had also seen Miss Baxter making furtive calls. At least to me they looked furtive. Snapping her phone shut when she had seen I was watching her. And I thought, what if she had a secret life, was an undercover agent, and she'd come to the school for some dark purpose? And then had to fake her own death so she could move on to her next assignment.

It was those 'what-ifs' that were always getting me into trouble. My imagination had caused me a mountain of problems at my last school.

I saw the French assistant, Mademoiselle Carlier, and the new science teacher going home together in her car one night after school. I had noticed them before, sharing a look, a smile when they thought no one was watching. But the science teacher was married.

'What if they're having an affair?' I whispered.

I whispered it to the wrong person. She passed it on and I was pulled into the head's office and warned about spreading rumours. That had been my first warning. The first of many.

But it was this story, this one in particular, my insistence that I had seen Miss Baxter, that had caused the most trouble. I wouldn't let it go. I wouldn't let them say I was making it up. I *had* seen her. It hadn't been a mistake. I began to get angry when people ridiculed me. And that just got me into more trouble.

My parents finally decided it would be best to take me out of that school and find somewhere else. It was a case of leaving before I was pushed. I was already on my final warning by this time. Unfair, in my opinion. I never caused real trouble. I wasn't a bully. I was never disruptive . . . I just noticed things other people missed. And, in the end, I had been right about Mademoiselle Carlier. Her and the science teacher had run off together, causing no end of scandal. But, of course, no one remembered that! Oh no. In fact, it only seemed to make things worse. As if by telling people about my suspicions I had actually made it happen. As if *I'd* done something wrong.

Sleekit, one of the teachers called me.

Sleekit. A great Scottish word – it means sly and underhand and untrustworthy. A great word, but not when it was applied to me. It hurt. I wasn't sleekit at all.

I had promised myself that here, in this new school, St Anthony's College, things were going to be different.

No more stories. I'd keep my imagination for the pages of my notebook. Here, I wanted to make a good impression. This was a clean slate, a new page.

So, why had I suddenly remembered seeing my dead teacher that day?

I shivered. The corridor grew colder. Didn't they say that happens when a ghostly presence is nearby? I pushed the thought away, determined my imagination would not ruin things for me again here.

2

I was sitting in the corridor outside the Rector's office. Mr Hyslop had popped his bushy head round the door only a few minutes ago. He had smiled at me through an equally bushy beard. 'I'll try not to keep you waiting too long, Tyler,' he had said. 'I have someone in with me at the moment.' And I had smiled back and nodded, quite happy to wait.

I looked up at the high, ornate ceilings, at the wooden pillars lining the walls. Angels had been carved into the dark wood. Angels with trumpets heralding Judgement Day, angels holding open prayer books, angels flying with outspread wings. Angels everywhere. There was a window near the roof, in the shape of a wheel, a beautiful stained-glass window depicting scenes from the Bible.

Another sudden cold shiver ran through me. It was the cold in this old school corridor, that was all, I told myself. Bone-snapping February cold.

At that moment, I wished Mum was here. She'd wanted to be. She had driven me right up the winding gravel drive to the entrance this morning, past a long line of elm trees and a mist-shrouded lake. She had almost begged to come in with me. She worries about me, especially since the dead teacher thing. That had really bothered Mum. I had seen her face crease with concern whenever I talked about it. She must have thought her only daughter was going crazy. I didn't want her to worry about me any more.

And anyway, her and Dad had already been to the school, checked it out, met up with the Rector. There was no need for her to come in with me this morning. I was a big girl now, I assured her. And I knew she was already late for work. 'I'll be fine, Mum,' I kept telling her. 'I'd much rather go in by myself.'

St Anthony's College seemed to loom over us as we came up the drive, its carved contours etched against the dark clouds.

'Isn't this is an imposing building?' Mum said.

I had to agree with her. St Anthony's was the kind of place that spun stories. It had originally been built as a boarding school for poor boys, and had been run by a religious order of monks. That had been way back in the 1800s. It was built of red brick that seemed to give out a sunset glow, even on a dark, misty morning like this. Almost as if it was lit from within. It had a gothic look, with arched windows and richly carved spires, and those wheel windows on either side of the elaborately decorated front doors. There were even gargoyles jutting out under the roofs. Red, devilish gargoyles, each one of their grotesque faces different. One grinning, one spitting, another with red fangs exposed ready to bite. And every one of those monstrous faces seemed to be watching me.

'They were supposed to frighten off evil spirits,' Mum told me. 'Keep them from entering the building.'

'I think it's working,' I told her. 'I don't want to go inside there myself now.'

And, though I was joking, the faces of those gargoyles did give me the creeps. It was as if they were warning me to stay away from here. Warning me that if I stepped inside that front entrance, bad things would happen.

Imagination! Tyler! I forced the thoughts back into the box. The box I had promised myself I would keep locked until I needed to open it for a story.

'Bit like Notre Dame, isn't it?' Mum said, breaking

into my dark thoughts.

She was right. That was exactly what it reminded me of. We'd been there, her and me, only last year. And the cathedral and the stories behind it had fired my imagination. Especially the gargoyles. Now here they were again, as if they'd followed me all the way from Paris. I was half expecting Quasimodo to appear between them, peering over the roof at me.

'I'll phone you at lunch, Mum,' I told her as I got out of the car. 'Tell you how I get on.'

'OK, honey,' Mum said. She even insisted on kissing me goodbye. I just hoped no one spotted her. But she's a brilliant mum. Dad's great too. Even after everything that I had put them through at my last school, they were right behind me. Didn't believe me either, of course. They thought it was only my vivid imagination playing tricks on me. They're so down to earth. Same with my big brother, Steven. He's training to be a car mechanic, like my dad, and you don't get more down to earth than that. Dad says he doesn't know where I get my imagination from. He says I come from a long line of car mechanics.

So, here I was, waiting for Mr Hyslop, on my own. Trying to rein in that imagination of mine. I looked around again at the high, ornate ceiling, at the wooden pillars, at the tall stained-glass windows. And I shivered again. As if icy cold fingers had tiptoed down my spine. It was only the cold, I told myself. There just wasn't enough heating in this big school.

I sat back in the uncomfortable plastic chair. A plastic chair. Here. It was totally out of place in these ancient and elaborate surroundings, and I looked at all the dark wood pillars again. At the saints and the angels, and the devils luring them into sin. No wonder this was a listed building. Couldn't be pulled down or altered. I could see why. All this could never be replaced.

Across from me there was a glass cabinet displaying all the sporting trophies the school has won over the years. Plaques and quaichs and shields. There was a photograph of Mr Hyslop, a younger Mr Hyslop, his hair not so grey, his wild beard black as coal, proudly holding a School Sports Championship trophy. From the newspaper article displayed below, it seemed Mr Hyslop had been a champion athlete himself in his younger days. There was a picture of the Pope on the wall above the cabinet. Which Pope I don't know. I'm not a Catholic, and actually, nowadays, neither is St Anthony's a Catholic school. Long ago it became not only co-educational, but non-denominational too. Up until about thirty years ago, though, it was still a residential school run by monks.

I looked at my watch. Mr Hyslop was taking his time. Teachers walked past me in the corridor. Some nodded and smiled. Others ignored me. The odd pupil slouched past.

I wondered if I would like it here. It was so different from my last school. That had been bright and modern, with wide spaces, and open staircases leading to the floors above. St Anthony's was dark and old, with alcoves and nooks and crannies and statues everywhere. The kind of school where you could imagine anything might happen . . .

Shut up, Tyler! There you go again. New beginning. Remember!

There was a statue standing on a plinth against the far wall. There seemed to be statues everywhere in St Anthony's. This one was holding a baby gently in his arms. One hand was raised in a benediction, and his eyes were looking down fondly at the baby.

I could hear chairs scraping across the floor inside Mr Hyslop's office, as if whoever was in there with him was standing up, getting ready to leave.

11

I stood up too and turned to the wall behind me. It was covered with framed photographs of graduating classes. They stretched right back to the early 1900s. Went from black and white to colour. In earlier years, the teachers had all been priests or monks. I wondered how many of those faces, priests and pupils, were still alive today. There were years when everyone looked so happy. 1950 they were throwing up their hands joyfully. But 1979 looked like a grim year. I looked closely at all the faces, pupils and teachers. There was a much younger Mr Hyslop again, but looking sullen this time. And there was a tall priest in black, his face set in a frown. Hardly a smile, in fact, from any of them, just steady gazes at the camera.

I turned back as I heard the handle of the door being opened just a fraction, as the Rector and his visitor finished their discussion.

'Yes, that will be absolutely fine. We'll get that sorted as soon as possible,' Mr Hyslop was saying.

Something drew my gaze back to the statue. What made me look up at his eyes? I don't know.

But they were no longer looking at the baby . . .

Now they were looking directly at me.

3

I stumbled back, fell against the chair and sent it crashing to the floor. My head cracked against the case that held the trophies. Blackness closed in around me. I was drowning in blackness. Like dark smoke swallowing me, till all I could see was the face of that statue, and those eyes staring right at me.

I came to, didn't know at first where I was, and the Rector, this Mr Hyslop, was standing above me, looking concerned. I was so glad he was blocking my view of the statue. I was too terrified to look at it again.

'What happened, Tyler?'

I could still see black spots in front of my eyes. My head ached. My first thought was to tell him. Blurt it all out. Point to the statue and yell, 'The statue moved. The eyes moved. The statue was looking at me.'

But what would he say to that? I could picture the look he would give me. I'd seen that look so many times on other teachers' faces.

'I saw Miss Baxter in the supermarket . . .'

'Don't be silly, Tyler. She's been dead for six months.'

I could still hear their cold voices, see their disbelieving eyes.

How could I possibly tell the Rector the statue had moved?

Mr Hyslop was waiting for an answer. 'Tyler? Shall I call the nurse?'

The last thing I wanted on my first day at the new school. 'I just fell.' I knew my voice trembled. I could feel cold sweat bead on my skin.

'You're very pale,' he said, helping me to my feet. 'Sure you'll be all right?

I moved with him inside his office, making sure his big form blocked my view.

'I think you should sit down for a bit. I'll take you up to your class shortly.'

I kept my eyes on the ground as I stepped behind him.

It was only your imagination, Tyler. I kept telling myself that. Over and over. *Your freaky imagination.*

I wanted this school to be different. Well, it was up to me to make things different. I would not let my imagination ruin things for me here.

Mr Hyslop brought me a glass of cold water, and motioned me very gently to the seat in front of his desk. On it was a brass plaque – *Dr Robert Hyslop. Rector.* Rector. It sounded so grand, so much grander than headmaster. I kept my eyes fixed on that plaque and barely listened as he explained about the school ethos and the rules, and how he hoped I would be happy here. And he asked me again and again if I was sure I was all right. He sounded genuinely concerned. I knew if I didn't pull myself together he would insist I go to the nurse. So I assured him, with a strained smile, that I felt fine. As if blacking out in school was something I did on a regular basis.

By the time he stood up to take me to my class, my head had stopped throbbing and I'd steeled myself to face that statue again.

Mr Hyslop moved aside so that I could leave the office before him. My eyes were drawn to the statue. I couldn't not look at it. My gaze moved slowly from the sandalled feet peeping out from under his long robe to his raised hand . . . and, finally, up to his face.

I gasped at the gentle eyes: they were resting on the baby again.

The Rector followed my gaze. 'St Joseph,' he explained. 'I hope you don't mind statues, Tyler. You'll find they're everywhere in St Anthony's. They're part of the school's heritage. The whole building is listed, so we try to keep everything intact. '

I only nodded and said nothing, and as we passed up the long, tiled corridor, there were statues on every side. Saints and monks and nuns and angels.

I would have to get used to them.

Anyway, it had only been my imagination. The kind eyes had only ever rested on the baby. Why would they look at me? How could he have moved? It was impossible.

By the time I walked into the classroom, I was determined to forget the incident. It was nonsense, I convinced myself. And I even managed a smile as Mr Hyslop introduced me to the teacher, Mr O'Hara.

He was a good-looking man, couldn't have been more much more than forty, with a thick mane of rich grey hair. Bet a lot of the older girls had a crush on him. He walked to the classroom door with Mr Hyslop and spoke for a whispered moment with him before he left.

Then he came back to me and smiled. 'So this is Tyler Lawless. Our new girl.' He turned to the class. 'Now I want you to make her feel very welcome.'

I looked round the classroom taking in all the faces. It was hard not to be drawn first to the raven-haired girl sitting in the front row. Her hair was too black to be natural, and it stood up in wayward spikes. Her eyebrow was pierced with a silver ring. She was biting on the end of a pen, and she had the greenest eyes I had ever seen. They were staring straight at me, sizing me up. She looked bold and a bit scary, and yet there was something I liked about her right off. And when I barely smiled at her, she flashed me a grin right back.

There was an Asian-looking boy sitting beside her, all gangly, and beside him a red-haired boy. He leaned across and whispered something and the Asian boy glanced at me, nodded and laughed. Were they laughing at me? I was sure they were. Why did I always think people were laughing at me? I hadn't done anything yet.

My eyes moved behind them to a fat boy who studied me with a cold stare. Right at the back, a pale-skinned boy just watched me curiously. An Asian girl caught my eye too. She wasn't the least bit interested in me. She couldn't take her eyes off the boys at the front.

Fancied one of them probably.

I took all this in while Mr O'Hara kept right on talking. Didn't listen to a word he was saying, so when he finished and said, 'So what do you think, Tyler?' I realised I didn't know what he was talking about. That's always my problem too. Letting my mind wander. Not listening.

I must have looked blank.

'Never mind.' He patted me on the shoulder. 'It's a lot to take in at once.'

He showed me my seat. It was in the row by the window and before too long I was forgotten. The lesson continued.

There were statues in this classroom too. A small one on the windowsill, and a larger one in the corner. I recognised this as St Francis. Everyone knows him. Birds on his shoulder, and on his outstretched hand. And by his feet, a fawn. I couldn't be afraid of him.

It made what I had imagined earlier seem even more stupid now.

As soon as the lesson ended, the spiky-haired girl came up to me, put a hand on my shoulder. 'So you took one look at old Hyslop and you fainted then?'

I was flabbergasted. 'How did you know?'

She laughed. 'Heard him whispering to O'Hara to keep his eye on you. You can't keep a secret in this place.' She giggled and nodded at the statue. 'Saw you staring at the statues. You're no' a Catholic?'

'No,' I said. 'But I don't mind the statues,' I added quickly. I didn't want to offend her.

'This is St Francis,' she informed me, touching his foot as she passed. I noticed that his foot was worn, as if many people had touched it before her.

'I know,' I said.

'I'll keep you right about the statues.' She grinned at me. 'I'm Jasmine, by the way,' she said. 'But everybody calls me Jazz.' She held out a packet of chewing gum. I took a piece just to be polite, and she popped another into her mouth.

'Jazz? That's nice.'

She flashed me another of those brilliant smiles and pulled the Asian girl towards her. 'This is Aisha.'

Aisha shrugged herself free. 'I can speak for myself, Jazz.' Then she smiled too. 'Aisha Saleem. Where did you get an exotic name like Tyler Lawless from?' She said it as if Aisha Saleem wasn't equally exotic.

'Yeah, wi' a name like that you should be a writer,' Jazz said.

I beamed at her. Couldn't help it. 'That's exactly what I want to be . . . a writer.'

As soon as I said it, I remembered I had promised myself not to tell anyone about my ambition in this school. It would be my secret. So much for that promise.

Jazz slipped her arm in mine. 'Great! At last, Aisha, somebody to help us with our English homework.'

She was pulling me along the corridor, which was jammed with pupils hurrying to their next class. 'Well, Tyler, if you're looking for a story, you came to the right school.' It was difficult to hear what she was saying there was so much noise. Yet, even as her voice became a whisper, I could suddenly make out every word. 'There was a murder here, years ago . . . in this school . . . and they never found the body.'

4

I wouldn't ask. I would pretend I wasn't the least bit curious, even though I was dying to know all about it.

A murder, at this school? A mystery, a body never found . . . a writer's dream.

But this was my new beginning. Things were going to be different, and if I showed too much interest they would begin to grow suspicious of me.

There was no more time to talk about it anyway. Rushing from one class to another, getting to know new teachers and classrooms. It was lunchtime before we had any chance to talk, and I promised myself I wouldn't be the first one to mention it.

Jazz collected her tray and swaggered down the school cafe. I followed in her wake. Everyone noticed her. She knew it. She expected it. She had so much confidence I envied her. Then she stopped at one of the tables and sprawled herself across it. 'Our table, Tyler,' she told me, and I was pleased that I was included in the 'our' she was talking about. She put down her tray and plonked herself on to a seat. 'Come on, Aisha!' she called out, and Aisha was there beside her.

'Do you think you'll like it here?' she asked me as she sat down.

'Yes, I hope so . . .' I looked around the cafe as I spoke.

'The school cafe'. The name didn't suit this dining hall. It was a massive room with high ceilings and tall windows and, even in here, more statues. An imposing stone fireplace dominated the room, and above it were words carved in an ancient script:

DOMINUS VOBISCUM

'It means "The Lord be with you",' Jazz said, following my gaze.

The plastic tables and chairs looked even more out of place here. There should have been long wooden tables in this hall, and high-backed oak chairs, and torches burning in brass holders on the walls. Once there would have been. I could imagine the candlelight flickering on the tables, almost hear the low hum of monks in prayer, picture row upon row of boys, heads bent, eating silently.

'Hi, Callum, come and join us.' Jazz broke into my thoughts. She was calling out to the fat boy as he walked past with his tray. He didn't have to be asked twice.

'Hi, Tyler, how's it going?' Callum asked.

'This here Callum,' Jazz said, poking Callum in the shoulder, 'is the smartest boy in the school . . . at least, according to him.'

Jazz laughed. So did Callum. 'Nothing wrong with blowing your own trumpet, eh, Tyler? So what are you good at?'

'Tyler's a writer,' Aisha said, before I could open my mouth to answer.

Callum leaned over the table at me, and I knew what he was going to say before he said it. 'You'll get a great story here. Have you heard about the murder?'

'Too late, Callum. I've told her all about it . . . you can add the gory details I missed later.' Jazz peered above my head. 'Oh, look, here come Laurel and Hardy.

Laurel and Hardy were the Asian boy and the red-head. They were heading right for us. As soon as they reached the table, they swung their legs over the chairs

anted their trays on the table, as if they were stak-
ing their claim. Seemed everyone was welcome at 'our'
table.

The redhead introduced himself. 'I'm Adam
Drummond. Sorry Jazz is the first person you've met in
the school. She always gives a bad impression.'

'Me and Aisha have been really nice, haven't we,
Tyler?'

I noticed then that Aisha's cheeks had flushed red.
She definitely fancied one of them.

'They've been great,' I said.

'As we always are,' Aisha said, trying to sound normal.

'This ugly-looking creature,' Adam punched the
Asian boy, 'is Mahmoud.' He pronounced Mahmoud as
if he belonged to a Scottish clan. MacDuff, Macleod,
Macmoud. 'But everybody calls him Mac.'

Mac suited him. He sounded more Scottish than
Adam. 'So, what do you think of it so far?'

Then both him and Adam said at once, 'Rubbish!'

Jazz raised her eyes. 'Just ignore them, Tyler. Hey,
what do you think of Mr O'Hara? Dishy, isn't he?'

'He is really good-looking, for an old guy,' I agreed.

Jazz pointed to her third finger, left hand. 'Have you
noticed his ring? Married. Very married.'

Callum spoke through a mouthful of broccoli. 'He was a pupil here at the time of the murder.'

'He was in the same class as the victim,' Jazz said. 'In fact, he was his best friend.'

'But they'd fallen out. I think it was over a lassie,' Mac said, then he added wisely, 'Lassies are nothing but trouble. O'Hara never talks about it anyway.'

Adam agreed. 'We asked him to tell us about it once but he just clammed up. "It's in the past" was all he would say.'

'Let the dead stay dead.' Mac put on an eerie voice.

'But they don't, do they? Not in this school.' Jazz leaned closer. 'The school's supposed to be haunted.'

'Don't tell me any more,' I wanted to say. But I couldn't find my voice. Couldn't stop listening.

'People have heard strange noises in the night,' Aisha said.

'Classroom doors opening of their own accord,' Callum added.

'Don't believe you,' I said. 'You're just trying to frighten me.'

Jazz shrugged. 'Ask the cleaners. They will only work in pairs in this school.'

'Yeah,' Adam agreed. 'They could tell you a thing or two about what goes on here.'

And I had to ask. Could not wait a moment longer. 'Who was murdered?'

Jazz answered me eagerly. 'One of the pupils. A boy. Ben Kincaid. They say he was a bad lot, always in trouble. Nobody really liked him. Not the teachers, not the pupils. Well, even his best mate had fallen out with him. And Mr O'Hara's really nice. He wouldn't fall out with anybody unless it was over something really serious. That tells you a lot, doesn't it?'

Callum took up the story. 'But one of the teachers . . . a priest, Father Michael, he was always on Ben Kincaid's case. Dragging him to the Rector's office. Ranting at him in the classroom. They hated each other. Ben Kincaid was always threatening to get him. And then somebody heard the priest say, "Not if I get you first." Everybody knew there was going to be trouble one day, and then, one night, it seems Ben Kincaid broke into the school. And Father Michael caught him. It was the last straw. The priest really lost it. Grabbed a knife and chased him to the old chapel.'

I looked at Jazz. 'The old chapel?'

'It's at the other end of the school. Very atmospheric,'

Jazz informed me. 'It's never used now.'

Callum broke in, a bit annoyed at being interrupted. 'Hey, who's telling this story!' Jazz just grinned and, after a pause, Callum went on. 'In the morning, all they found was blood on the chapel floor, but no Ben Kincaid.'

'And they never found his body?' I asked.

'Never.'

'Searched everywhere,' Mac added. 'Even dragged the lake.' He looked to the windows then, as if we could see the lake from there. Through the thick walls, through the trees. But I could picture it. I had noticed it this morning through the line of elms as Mum drove us up the long gravel drive to the school. A morning mist hovered over the dark water and I'd thought even then it looked mysterious.

'But they never found Ben Kincaid,' Mac said.

By this time I was completely caught up in the story. 'Maybe he just ran away.'

'They thought of that. But Kincaid had a mother,' Jazz said. 'She was dying about him, spoiled him rotten. They say that was half his problem. He got everything he wanted from his mum. So, why would he run away and not get in touch with her?'

Aisha said softly, 'People say the poor woman died of a broken heart just a year after the murder.'

'She was run over by a bus, Aisha!' Mac said.

Aisha shook her head. 'They say she walked in front of it. Couldn't face life any more.' She let out a big sigh of empathy for the 'poor woman'.

'They found Father Michael in his study the morning after the murder. His face was ashen,' Jazz said dramatically. 'There was blood on his robes, Ben Kincaid's blood. And it turned out the knife that killed Ben Kincaid was in his pocket. His fingerprints were all over it.'

'What they call an open and shut case.' Jazz counted on her fingers. 'Motive, means and opportunity.'

'Did he confess?'

Jazz shook her head. 'Nope. Never did. All he said was, "I am innocent." Said he'd found the knife in the old chapel. But he was arrested and found guilty. He died in prison, still saying he was innocent. Nobody believed him.'

'And now he haunts the school?' I said.

'Nobody knows who haunts the school.'

'I think it's just draughty myself,' Mac said.

'All a load of rubbish,' Callum said. 'And, as Jazz

pointed out, I am the smartest boy in the school.'

Everyone laughed.

'I have sensed things,' Jazz said, and I wondered if she was winding me up.

'Have you?' I asked.

'Oh yeah, I'm very open to suggestion.'

'Well, I suggest you shut up,' Mac said, and after that it all descended into jokes and fun and laughter.

I still wasn't sure if they'd made the whole thing up, taking the mickey, in a nice way, out of the new girl. But as I left the school that day and I passed the corridor where Mr Hyslop's office was, I steeled myself and cast a glance at St Joseph. His hand raised in prayer. The child still in his arms, and his eyes . . . I let out a long sigh of relief. His eyes were set on the baby.

All my imagination, I told myself. By tomorrow, I would have forgotten all about it.

5

'You made friends then? Your first day? I'm so pleased about that,' Mum said.

I'd had to go over my whole day for Mum and Dad that night at dinner. I knew they so much wanted things to work out for me in this school. So I told them all the things they wanted to hear. How helpful the teachers were, who was in my class. Told them about Jazz and Aisha and the boys too. I told them everything, except about the murder. And of course, I didn't mention the fact I had knocked myself out in the first five minutes of being there. And I certainly didn't say anything about the statue. Especially not to Mum. It seemed to really freak her out that I thought I had seen someone who was dead. To tell her a statue had moved? That was even more spooky.

'They made me feel as if I'd been their friend for ages.'

'Well, you'd do the same for a new girl, wouldn't you? You're a nice, friendly girl yourself, Tyler.' Dad beamed at me. I could wind Dad round my finger like a piece of string. He would say that with my fair hair and blue eyes I looked like an angel. His little angel, he called me. And Steven would remind him that the devil had been an angel too. Lucifer.

'You're better off out of that other school. You let your imagination run away with you there,' Dad said. 'You keep out of trouble in this school, and you'll be fine.'

Of course, he was right. I *had* let my imagination run away with me in the other school.

Miss Baxter was dead. There are no such things as ghosts. And statues can't move.

End of story.

Over the next couple of days it seemed there was nothing for me to worry about anyway. I got to know more people in my class, from the friendly to the not so friendly. The morose girl who sat beside me never smiled once and complained about everything. The pale boy at the back of the class never spoke a word, always sitting in silence. And he never seemed to take his eyes off me. There was another boy with dark hair who was always bent across his desk. I hadn't even seen his face yet. I think he was asleep half the time. I couldn't get their names sorted out in my head. Not yet.

I began to fit in. I felt as if I had been there for ever.

'So, which one do you fancy?' I asked Aisha one day, just as Adam and Mac had walked past us and her cheeks had flushed bright red again.

She was totally shocked by the question. 'I don't fancy either of them,' she insisted. 'I'm too busy to think about boys!'

'Come on, Aisha, you can tell me!' Jazz called out to her as she stormed off. 'I'm your best friend.'

Aisha ignored her. Jazz slipped her arm in mine. 'Who says we'll make it our life's mission to find out which one it is? My money's on Mac.'

'I don't know, Jazz. There's something really cute about Adam.'

Now she was the one who was shocked. 'Stands back in amazement! Don't tell me you fancy *him*?'

'No. Don't be daft. I'm only saying . . . it just might be Adam. A lot of the girls in school fancy him.'

Jazz looked even more staggered. 'He's a ginger!' she snapped.

I smiled. 'He's a gorgeous ginger.' I had seen that written in black above the mirror in the toilets.

Adam the gorgeous ginger

And there *was* something roguish about Adam. The kind of boy you could imagine as a highwayman, or a cowboy, or a buccaneer.

'Adam!' Jazz dragged me on. 'If it is Adam, I am having Aisha analysed.'

So the days went on and I forgot about murder and ghosts and the statue that had moved . . .

Until, that is, the day that Mr O'Hara sent me to collect some books he had left in the library on the first floor.

6

It was a dark day. Rain battered against the stained-glass windows, mist cloaked the stark trees in the grounds and hung over the lake. I left the classroom, assuring Mr O'Hara that I knew where to go. I'd never been in the school library but I had passed it on the way to other classes. I was rather pleased that he'd asked me, out of the whole class, to run this errand for him.

I barely glanced at the statues as I passed them on my way up the corridor. In fact, it wasn't until I reached the upper floor that I even thought about them.

But it was darker here, and the stained glass sent shafts of eerie green and red lights along the floor and up the walls. The only sounds I could hear were my own footsteps.

It's a curse having an imagination like mine. I tried to push it down, stifle it. Lock it in that box again.

Determined only to concentrate on the library door at the end of the corridor.

The library seemed to be guarded by the statue of a long dead cardinal, his hands clasped around a Bible. *Pray for me*, I thought, as I passed him. For I felt as if the dark, grey day was closing in on me.

I knocked on the door but there was no answer. Finally, I pushed it open and stepped inside. Here, in the library, there were more wooden pillars lining the walls, holding up the ornate ceiling.

'Mrs Devoy?' I called out for the librarian and my voice seemed to echo into the high roof. There was no answer. There was no one but me in the library. The books Mr O'Hara had asked me to collect were on a table by the door, just as he'd said. I picked them up but I didn't want to take them without letting Mrs Devoy know I'd been there. I walked between the bookshelves to the study room at the back of the library.

I pushed open the door. 'Mrs Devoy?'

You know when a room is empty, don't you? You know when there is no one but you there.

No one but me.

The library grew darker. Heavy grey clouds seemed to settle themselves in the sky; the wind whined through the old windows.

No statues at least in here, I thought.

Only wooden bookshelves and stacks of books, and pillars that stretched to the ceiling. Carved at the top of each pillar was an angel. Some praying and looking up to heaven, others gazing down to earth. Some with fingers twined and yet others with their hands held open.

I looked up to the top of one pillar. This angel seemed to be watching the door, as if she too was waiting for Mrs Devoy to come back. Her hands were held together. Fingers linked.

There was a footstep in the corridor. I was sure I heard it. Mrs Devoy, perhaps, on her way here. I looked quickly at the door, waiting for it to open, and the librarian to step inside, laden with books. The only way I ever saw her.

No one came in. The door stayed shut. There was no other sound. And after a moment, I looked back to the angel.

And she was staring at me.

At me.

This wasn't a mistake. She was looking right at me. Her blank eyes seemed alive. And her hands were no longer linked in prayer. They were open, her fingers stretched towards me. I began to tremble. It seemed the library was growing darker by the second. And I turned my eyes, my terrified eyes, on the angels at the top of each of the pillars.

They were all looking at me.

Every angel eye had searched me out.

Every angel eye was watching me.

I backed away. I wanted to call again for the librarian, scream for her, but my voice was stuck in my throat.

All I wanted was out of that library.

I grabbed at the brass handle of the door and pulled. It seemed stiff and for another terrified moment I was sure I wouldn't be able to get it open. I'd be trapped in there. I didn't even dare look back. So afraid those angels would suddenly wrench themselves from the pillars and fly towards me.

At last, I managed to prise the door open, and I stumbled back into the corridor. I was sure the statue of the cardinal outside the library had been looking up to heaven. Now, his head was bent towards me. His eyes looked alive now, and they were watching me. He seemed to have moved closer too. He was no longer holding the Bible. His stone hand was held out, his finger pointing.

Impossible.

He hadn't moved.

This couldn't be happening.

It was as if dusk had fallen in the corridor. The long grey shadows, turning to black, were edging closer. One of the books slipped from my hands, dropped to the floor. I bent to pick it up. Something moved close by me. Some kind of shadow. I bit at my lip. It was only a cloud passing the window; I kept telling myself that's what it was. A cloud passing the window. But as I looked up, the corridor seemed to stretch into the shadowy distance. Something was scratching at the windows. Like someone with long-nailed fingers trying to get in.

It's only the trees brushing against the glass, I yelled silently. *This isn't happening*. Why couldn't I scream? I turned back to the statue. Couldn't stop myself . . . His eyes had followed me, were still watching me, and his hands had moved again. They were held out to me, as if he was offering me something.

No!

I turned again and began to run.

No! His hands had always been like that. He had always been facing this way. The angels hadn't been looking at me. I was imagining it. Seeing things that weren't there.

All I wanted was to get back to the class, my friends, company.

There was a statue at the top of the stairs. I would have to pass it. St Teresa, Jazz had informed me when I had asked her. She had always looked so gentle, with closed eyes, absorbed in prayer. As I ran towards her, I looked up.

And her eyes were open. She was looking down at me too. Watching me.

I tried to draw in great gulps of air, and yet I could hardly breathe.

At the top of the stairs, I dared a look back at the line of statues along the corridor. And all the eyes had turned to me. They were all watching me, their hands all held out to me.

They had moved. I was sure of it now. And if I went back into that library those angels would be watching me too. Maybe even now loosening themselves from their wooden pillars, getting ready to fly out of the library and down this corridor towards me.

It was all too much, too much for anyone to take in. I screamed, took a step back and began to tumble down the stairs.

7

Jazz was staring down at me when I opened my eyes. Behind her, looking concerned, were Mr O'Hara and the rest of the class.

'What happened, Tyler?' Jazz asked.

I blinked, trying to get her into focus. They all seemed to be swimming in and out of my vision. The whole class was there. Adam, and Mac, and Callum and Aisha and the pale boy and the sullen girl. All watching me.

Jazz looked round at them. 'Move back, move back. Give her some breathing space here.'

Jazz was born to give orders. They all moved, except for Mr O'Hara.

'Can you stand up?' he asked.

'Of course I can,' I wanted to say. I wasn't hurting anywhere. Why couldn't I say a word?

I knew the answer. I was afraid of what I might say if I did speak. Of what I wanted to say. What I wanted to tell them.

The statues moved. They're alive. The angels in the library are alive.

I could see the statue behind Mr O'Hara. St Teresa. Her eyes were closed again. Not a glance at me. Uninterested.

I'd be accused of lying if I told anyone about them. No one would believe me.

Jazz helped me up.

'I think I should take her along to the medical room, sir,' she suggested, as if she was a teacher too. 'This isn't the first time she's fainted.'

'I think that's a good idea, Jasmine.'

Mac was watching me as we passed him. I'd never noticed before how brown his eyes were. 'Not the first time you've fainted, eh, Tyler. Going to get a reputation if you don't watch out.' He was smiling, but there was something in the smile I didn't like.

I spoke at last. 'I fell. I tripped. Couldn't help it.' The words tumbled out. Sounded like a lie even to me.

Jazz pulled me on. 'He's winding you up. Don't listen to him. Here, have some gum.' She offered it as if it were some kind of medicaton that would make me feel better.

I shook my head. 'Don't want any.'

As I hobbled along to the medical room. Jazz asked me again, 'What happened?'

I longed to tell her. I liked Jazz. Knew she liked me. But could I trust her? Trust her not to think I was an idiot. Trust her to believe me?

Not worth the risk, I decided.

'My imagination,' I said. 'I was hurrying along that corridor, and suddenly realised how dark and eerie it was . . . I looked back and lost my footing. That's all.'

It sounded so logical it could be the truth. I almost believed it myself.

Jazz looked disappointed. 'Aw, I see. I thought it might have been something else.'

'Something else? What else could it have been?' I wondered then if she'd seen the statues move too. I wanted so much for her to say it. Because then, both of us couldn't be wrong, could we?

Jazz blew a bubble. She waited till it burst before she answered me. 'Just thought you might have seen the ghost.'

8

I didn't tell Mum or Dad about the fall. When I got home, all the talk in the house was about some local girl who had gone missing. The papers were full of it, and it was the lead story on the regional news on television too. She lived not far from our house.

Anyway, there was nothing really to tell. I wasn't hurt. I only had a bruise on my shin you could hardly see. I didn't want anything to worry them. I would keep my imagination for my stories.

That gave me the idea. If this was one of my stories, what would I have the character do next?

Well, I thought, she'd look into the history of the college, see if anyone else had ever claimed that the statues came alive. Had seen the statues watching them. Surely that shouldn't be too difficult?

This was an old school, with a murky history. Strange

things must have been seen before by other people. And hadn't Jazz and the others said there was a ghost?

I began that very night, sitting at my computer, searching the internet. But the school's official website wanted to attract pupils, not put them off by informing them of strange and mysterious stories from its disturbing past.

It was only when I logged on to another website that I found what I wanted. It gave graphic details of the murder, and of Father Michael. There was a photograph of him. A faded black and white print. A tall, thin priest, all in black, with a stern face and hooded eyes. I remembered seeing him in one of the photographs, outside the Rector's office that first day with that same grim expression. He looked sinister. I could imagine him stalking the corridors of St Anthony's at midnight. Almost hear the swish of his robes. The story said Ben Kincaid, the boy, had sneaked back into the school to vandalise, to steal, and Father Michael had found him, confronted him.

But Ben had taunted him, as it seemed Ben Kincaid had taunted all the teachers, and that had sent the priest over the edge of reason. Father Michael had snatched up a knife and Ben had run. The priest had followed him relentlessly. I could almost see it happening. Every day I walked those long, dark corridors; it wasn't difficult to imagine Ben hurrying through the deserted school, realising this time he had gone too far. The only sound he could hear as he ran was the footfall of the priest close behind him.

Ben Kincaid grew more terrified by the second. Trying each door in turn, pulling at them, finding doors locked, windows tight shut. In his panic he ran to the one place there was no escape from . . . the chapel. Only one door. No other exit. Yet, this should surely have been the one place he'd be safe.

Sanctuary.

Once inside a church even criminals were meant to be safe . . . especially from a priest.

As I read on, it was as if I was back there, hurrying through those long winding corridors, looking around for a way out, as if I was running alongside Ben Kincaid. I pictured him stumbling into the chapel, searching for a place to hide. And there was nowhere. I saw him crouch down at the foot of a statue in the old chapel, trying to squeeze himself behind it. And all the time those footsteps were coming ever closer.

I was as afraid as Ben Kincaid must have been. I had

never been so afraid. Never wanted so much to live.

But it was too late. Because the chapel doors suddenly flew open. The hinges shook. Wood cracked. And there he was, filling the doorway. Father Michael. I saw the knife glint in his hand. Two strides and he would be on me, two strides and his hand is raised, and . . .

I leapt back from the screen, sweat pouring from me.

It was one thing to empathise with a victim, but this was something more than empathy. It was as if I had been there, seen it all. As if I had been, for that moment, Ben Kincaid. And it scared me.

I was afraid after that to look back at the screen. It took me a while to go back to the computer, close that website and skip away from the grisly details of the murder.

I wanted to know about the statues, the ghost. But no matter how many websites I visited, there were no reports of a haunting. Or any other strange happenings at St Anthony's. No sounds in the corridors, no footsteps in the night, no statues with a life of their own.

It seemed I was alone.

9

My friends had told me the school was haunted. Had they only been joking? I had to find out. Next day, I asked Jazz why she'd thought I had seen a ghost.

She shot forward in her seat. 'Did you!'

'No, of course, I didn't. But what made you think I did? Has anyone seen a ghost before?'

Callum blew out his cheeks in disgust. 'No. If this place is haunted, it's the most boring haunting in the world. Nobody's ever seen a thing.'

But I saw Jazz lift an eyebrow when he said that. 'Do you know different, Jazz?' I asked her.

Her cheeks flushed. 'I don't believe in any of that stuff. But somebody did see something, years ago, before our time. I heard about it.'

Mac entered the conversation. 'I never heard about any of this. Who was this?'

Aisha nudged him. 'What was his name again, Jazz? Loney, or something funny like that.'

'First name was Bill . . . that was it. He was expelled, remember?'

Mac looked puzzled. 'Him that was expelled for stealing? He'd just come out of borstal or something. Nobody would have believed him anyway.'

'That's what I mean,' Jazz said. 'Nobody believed him. He was a bad lot. But he said he saw things.'

'What kind of things?' I asked.

Jazz gazed at me. 'You did see something, didn't you?'

It was on the tip of my tongue to tell her, but Mac broke in. 'Oh, come on, don't ask her that! She'll jump at the chance to say she saw a ghost.'

'What are you saying that for?' I snapped at him.

He only tutted and moved back. As if he was fed up with me.

But of course, that decided me. I couldn't tell them anything. I shook my head. I might tell Jazz, or Aisha, but never Mac. Not after that. 'I just like ghost stories, that's all.'

Jazz almost whispered, 'The cleaners will only work in twos in this school, did you know that?'

'You told me that before.'

'It's true,' Jazz said. 'If anybody has seen anything weird happening in here, when this school is empty, it has to be them. They say that boy was telling the truth.'

'Yeah,' Aisha agreed. 'I've heard the cleaners say . . . they've seen a lot of strange things happening in this school at night time.'

Mac and Adam put on creepy voices. '*When . . . it's . . . daaark . . .*'

I didn't ask any more. The boys would have made a fool of me.

But I knew I couldn't let it go. A boy who was expelled, who had seen things? Cleaners with strange stories? I made my mind up. I was going to speak to the cleaners, see what I could find out.

It was easy to find an excuse to stay after school and speak to them. I would pretend I'd lost my bracelet when I fell down those stairs.

That same day instead of heading home, I made my way along the empty corridors to their room. I had waited till Jazz and Aisha had left the building. They would probably laugh at me too, or ask me more questions, or want to come with me. And this was something I had to do alone.

The women, there were three of them, were all crammed into a tiny room, getting ready to start work when I arrived.

'And where do you think you lost this bracelet?' one of them asked me. She said her name was Myra.

'I think it might have been on the upper floor, near the library. I fell, you see. Who is it cleans there?'

'Mrs Sorenson over there,' Myra said. She pointed to a big woman bending over pulling something out of her bag. All I could see was her butt.

'Mrs Sorenson works there on her own?' I asked innocently. 'I heard that the cleaners will only work in twos up there.'

Myra snorted. 'Och, are you a new lassie? Bet your pals told you that.'

She let out a cackle of laughter and nudged the woman beside her. 'Hear that, Ella. We're scared to work on our own.' She turned back to me. Her smile faded. I hoped I hadn't offended her. 'Think we're a bunch o'wimps? We're no' frightened to go anywhere in this school,' she said. 'Don't care what kind of noises I hear.'

'So . . . you do hear noises?' I sounded eager, I knew I did.

'This is an old school, wi' draughty, rattling windows. Of course you hear noises. But nothing supernatural.' The woman, Ella, answered me this time.

Mrs Sorenson came over then. 'Aye, Ella, you were quick enough to ask to be moved when you came here. Away from that upper floor.'

Ella snapped back at her. 'But nothing to do wi' a ghost. It's my arthritis. It kills me going up the stairs.'

I asked Mrs Sorenson. 'Do you hear things up there?'

She looked at me boldly. 'Oh aye, I've heard things.'

Ella tutted when she said that.

'Yes, I have!' Mrs Sorenson insisted. 'I think somebody's behind me and then when I turn . . . there's nobody there.'

'Don't listen to her, hen,' Myra said. 'She's winding you up.'

'You just heard things . . . you've never seen anything?' I asked her.

'The spirits haven't been able to materialise for me,' Mrs Sorenson said.

At this, Myra started to laugh. So did Ella. 'You see, hen, Mrs Sorenson here considers herself something of a medium. So she stays on the upper floor hoping Father Michael'll come walking through the walls and she can start charging money for his messages from the other side.'

Mrs Sorenson waved a mop threateningly. 'That's a lie! Take that back.'

She turned to me then. 'But, if there was a ghost to see up there, I would have seen it.'

'What about Ben Kincaid? Isn't he supposed to haunt the school?'

There was another snort. This time from Mrs Sorenson. 'Let me tell you, if that Ben Kincaid came back here to haunt this school, I'd blinking well give him a good wallop wi' my mop, and send him back where he came from.'

Ella joined in. 'Aye, his poor mother. He ruined her life.'

'It wasn't his fault he was killed,' I reminded them.

'Wasn't it?' Myra didn't seem convinced about that. 'Drove that Father Michael to it, that's what I think.'

'Still, Myra . . . that priest must have been a serial killer at heart to do what he did.' Ella looked at me. 'Blood everywhere, they said. Footsteps in blood leading back to Father Michael's study. His footsteps.' She looked round at her friends. 'Oh, I wouldn't have liked to be the one to clean that mess up.'

'If anywhere was going to be haunted, it would be that old chapel. That's where it happened.' This was from Myra.

'And nothing's ever happened there?' I asked.

Mrs Sorenson answered me. 'I'm the one that cleans in there. And it's only an old chapel. Let me tell you, I'm very sensitive to spirit. I would know.'

Myra and Ella couldn't stop laughing at this.

Mrs Sorenson glared daggers at them. 'Yes, I am!' she insisted. Then she looked back at me. 'Don't let your pals tell you this school is haunted.'

But I knew something they didn't. Strange things *were* happening here. But it seemed they were *only* happening to me.

Myra stood up ready to leave. 'I don't know why that chapel hasn't been pulled down. Old Hyslop wants to pretend the murder never happened. But he still wants the chapel preserved exactly the way it was. Blinkin' weirdo, him.'

Ella stood up too. 'It's a listed building. He's not got any choice. They can't touch anything in it.' She looked at me and smiled. A smile that changed her from a crabby old woman to someone's attractive mother. 'So, we've got to disappoint you, hen. No ghosts in this school.'

I gave it one last shot. 'Wasn't there a boy who was expelled . . . he saw things, didn't he?'

Ella stopped. 'And what was his name?'

Mrs Sorenson said, 'It was the boy Loney, wasn't it?'

I nodded. 'That was his name.'

Myra looked round at the others. She smiled. 'And can you remember his first name, hen?'

'Bill, Bill Loney,' I said.

Now they all laughed. 'And that's exactly what your pals were telling you, hen. A load of Bill Loney!'

Mrs Sorenson said kindly, 'Listen, love, when somebody new starts in this school, they're always wound up about the place being haunted. And they always get sent to us . . . with the Bill Loney story. The boy who was expelled because he saw strange things. And it's all ba-loney.'

I sighed. I felt so stupid. How could I have fallen for that one!

But on the other hand, Jazz and Aisha didn't know that I *had* seen things. Had I really been the only one?

'The statues are kind of creepy,' I said, following the cleaners out the door.

Mrs Sorenson nodded her head. 'Aye, you're right there. I walk along that corridor and I'm sure they're watching me and then I swivel round and . . .'

I drew in my breath. 'And what are they doing?'

Mrs Sorenson looked at me as if I was a wee bit crazy. 'Well, not a lot . . . they're only made of plaster.'

Ella started laughing then. 'What did you expect them to be doing? The Highland fling?'

Then they were all laughing. Patting me on the back, telling me to go back and think of a way I could wind up my friends now.

'You go back and tell your pals you have seen a ghost. Scare the life out of them. OK!' And I laughed too and left them.

I felt better after I spoke to them. Because it was all a wind-up. A load of baloney! What an idiot I was. There were no ghosts in the school. Everything had a logical explanation. And looking back at all that had happened, it seemed unreal now. As if it had been part of a dream. Not real at all. I had only imagined I had seen statues moving, and the story of an old murder mystery had done the rest.

10

It was growing dark as I wound my way out of the school. I had forgotten how dark it could be in February. And by now, the lights had been switched off in all the corridors. Mr Hyslop was trying to save electricity as well as the planet. I turned a corner and I could no longer hear the laughter of the cleaners. The dark panelled walls closed in. I felt completely alone. I hurried towards the main entrance, refusing to let my imagination go haywire again. Darkness seemed to fold around me.

No one in the corridor. Only me. Only my footsteps. Or . . . were there more? Footsteps following me?

I stopped, and the other footsteps stopped too. An echo, must have been an echo. No one was following me.

Pull yourself together, Tyler!

Somewhere behind me, out of sight, were the cleaners. Down-to-earth, happy women. Not afraid to be alone here. Nothing had ever happened to them . . . even working on their own at night in those empty classrooms. In that empty chapel where a murder had been committed, nothing ever happened to them. Why should I think anything would happen to me?

I would not look at the statues. I dared not.

They were made of plaster. They couldn't move. Of course they couldn't move.

Yet, I felt them all watching me. I was sure as soon as I walked past them their eyes followed my progress. If I swung round, I would catch them with their faces, their eyes, all turned towards me.

The front entrance seemed miles away. Seemed to be moving further away as I quickened my pace towards it. It was as if I was in a dream and would never get out of here. Never.

There were two statues by the front door. One on either side of the entrance. I would have to pass them. I wished now I'd asked one of the cleaners to walk me out of the school. Pretend I was so new I might get lost.

In the same second I yelled at myself not to be such a wimp. Told myself again the statues were made of plaster. They never moved for the cleaners, why should they move for me?

My imagination. I closed my fist and let my nails dig into my palms. All my imagination!

What made me glance up at the statue of St Martin? I couldn't stop myself. He was looking down at me, his hand pointing back along the corridor behind me, as if he was telling me to go back. Warning me not to leave. As if he wasn't going to let me pass. But I'd noticed his gentle face before, and it was always turned the other way . . . wasn't it?

I stopped dead. Terrified to pass him. Only my breathing filled the dark silence. I began to back against the wall.

And felt a cold hand touch my shoulder.

11

'Why are you still here, Tyler?'

It was Mr Hyslop. I managed to stifle a scream. He looked stern. 'What are you doing in the school at this time?'

'I lost my bracelet, sir. I was asking the cleaners to look out for it.' The lie sounded believable though my voice trembled.

He shook his head. 'I was hoping you would tell me the truth. No, you weren't, Tyler. I overheard you speaking to them. Why are you so interested in Ben Kincaid?'

'It's . . . it's an interesting story, sir . . .' I could hardly speak. He must have heard everything.

'And this school is not haunted,' he said sternly. 'I heard the cleaners tell you that. And no spreading any stories about you seeing ghosts.' He waved a finger at me. It was stained with nicotine. 'I will come down on you like a ton of bricks, if I hear anything like that, Tyler.'

I wanted to say it wasn't fair. I'd been told the school was haunted. Jazz had told me. But it seemed like a betrayal to tell him that.

'You write stories, I know that,' he went on. 'Well, keep your imagination for those stories. The murder of Ben Kincaid was a dark time in the school's history. We try to forget about it here. I suggest you do too.'

'Yes, sir.'

He managed a small smile. Forced it. 'Although I'll bet it was those girls put you up to it. That Jasmine especially. Told you the old story about the place being haunted, I suppose.'

I kept my eyes on the floor.

'Well, as the cleaners told you, there are no ghosts here. Never have been, never will be. And that's the last I want to hear about it. OK?'

I only nodded.

That seemed to satisfy him. 'Come on, I'll walk down the drive with you. It's too dark for you to walk there on your own. This missing girl is making everyone nervous.'

Debbie Lawson. Everyone knew her name now, as if they had met her, knew her. Her photo was on television every night. Last seen wearing a pink jacket.

I found my voice at last. 'But she's only run away, hasn't she, sir? She hasn't been abducted or anything.'

'I don't think the police are ruling out anything. Better not take any chances,' he said.

As we walked down the long drive to the gates, I was glad of his company, even with that stern expression on his face. He was old, but he was still a big, powerful man. I remembered the school trophies outside his office. He had helped the school teams win rugby competitions and marathons. He would be a match for anyone who might leap out of those trees.

Anyone human, that is.

Or alive.

It wasn't only dark. The mist from the lake seemed to drift through the trees as if it had a life of its own.

'The bus stop's at the bottom of the road. I'll wait with you till the bus comes.'

'Thank you, sir.' A kind man, I thought, in spite of his anger at my questioning the cleaners.

'Are you liking it here, Tyler?'

'Yes, sir.' It was no lie. I did like the school and the

friends I had made. I was just terrified of something that lurked in here . . . or did it only lurk in my imagination? I went on, 'I think it will be really nice in the summer.'

'Why in the summer?'

'It's a bit creepy in the dark winter days, sir.'

He looked across at the lake, cloaked in mist. 'Yes, I suppose it is. I've always found it atmospheric.' His face creased into a smile.

I wanted to ask him more. What Father Michael was like. Was he as cruel as they all said? Mr Hyslop had been here when the murder took place. But he'd told me he never wanted to hear of it again. I could understand that. This was *his* school. The murder was all in the past. Best forgotten.

I thought so too. I only prayed that the past would forget about me.

12

Jazz phoned me that night, all giggles. 'We saw you going to see the cleaners. Knew you'd do that.'

'That was so cruel. I felt so daft, Jazz. Bill Loney! How could I fall for that!'

She giggled again. 'We were waiting for you, outside the front door, but then we saw old Hyslop and made a run for it. What did he say?'

Well, I could wind people up too. 'He said he knew you and Aisha were behind it. He didn't blame me at all. He's going to have a stern word with you tomorrow.'

For once Jazz was lost for words. There was a stunned silence on the line. 'I don't believe it! I'm always the one that ends up in trouble.'

I was going to tell her I was only kidding, but decided against it. One night of worry wouldn't do her any harm.

*

And so one dark February day followed another. Statues stayed still and silent. Once again I pushed the things I imagined I had seen to the back of my mind. It was over.

The most important thing in those next few days for me and Jazz was finding out who it was Aisha fancied.

'I saw her in the córridor with Adam,' I told Jazz. We were in class waiting for Mr O'Hara to arrive. 'All giggles, she was flirting like mad.'

Jazz disagreed. 'Trying to make Mac jealous. Have you seen the way she looks at him? Talk about fluttering your eyelashes. She practically causes a hurricane.'

'Why doesn't she just tell us?' I wondered.

Jazz had an easy answer. 'Would you admit to fancying one of them?'

I didn't want to admit that I thought both of them were OK. Better than OK. Mac with those dark chocolate eyes and Adam with his red hair and mischievious grin.

'By the way,' Jazz said, 'Mr Hyslop pulled me and Aisha aside this morning. Warned us about filling your head with nonsense about ghosts and murder. You know what I almost said . . .' I waited. 'I almost told him it wasn't nonsense about the murder. I mean it did happen.

Are we not supposed to mention it?!' She pursed her lips as if she was really annoyed. But I was getting to know Jazz. She had too much of a sense of humour to get annoyed at anything.

I noticed that the silent boy at the back of the class had leaned forward as if he was listening, and trying to pretend he wasn't. What was his name again? And why was he always staring at me ? I decided to ask Jazz.

'See that boy at the back . . . he's always looking at me . . . I can never remember his name.'

Jazz giggled. 'Maybe he fancies you? Who do you mean?' She turned right round to look, but just then, the door was flung open, and Mr O'Hara almost fell into the classroom laden with books.

Jazz called out to him. 'Mr O'Hara, Tyler here wants to know why we're not allowed to ask about the murder.'

I tried to slide under the desk. A flush came to the teacher's face. 'That is not a subject for discussion, Jasmine.'

'But I mean, sir, you can't blame her for being interested.'

I tried to pretend I was invisible.

'The school could be making loads of money out of

this, sir. Murder tours round St Anthony's . . . a bit like the ones they do in Edinburgh,' Adam shouted. 'Or even ghost tours . . . if we had a ghost, that is.'

'Why *is* this school *not* haunted, sir?' Callum asked in a deep imposing voice, as if it was a question he'd been pondering for a long time. 'I mean, we've had a murder . . . but no a sign of a ghost.'

The teacher dropped the books on his desk. 'And a very good thing too, Callum.'

'You were here when the murder took place, weren't you, sir?' It was Mac who asked him. 'Ben Kincaid was your best friend, wasn't he?'

I saw the teacher's face grow pale at the memory. Did no one else notice that?

'You would think,' Mac went on, 'that Ben Kincaid might have been a bit miffed at getting murdered and come back to let *you* especially know how annoyed he was.'

Bold as brass, Jazz called out to him, 'Tell us about the murder, sir.'

His eyes were cold when he looked back at her. 'A murder is no cause for entertainment, Jasmine. It was a tragedy. A tragedy for a lot of people.'

'Especially for Ben Kincaid,' Mac muttered.

'Yes,' Mr O'Hara said. 'And for his mother, and for Father Michael . . . and for the whole school, and that is all I am prepared to say about it. Don't ever ask me again.'

'You and him had a fight, didn't you, sir? Just before he was killed.'

Mr O'Hara's face went red. I saw his hands balled into fists on the desk, the knuckles white. He wanted to stop talking about this. He looked up sharply at Mac. 'Read about it on Wikipedia, did you? Well, Ben Kincaid had a fight with just about everybody at some point.' He bent back over his books. I had never seen him look angry. Mr O'Hara was always even-tempered and happy. But talking about Ben Kincaid . . . and being reminded of a fight he had had with him had made him lose his composure. I could see the muscles in his jaws clench and unclench as if he was struggling to hold in his anger.

Jazz whispered to me, 'Must be hard to lose your best friend like that. Especially when you've had a fight with him.'

Mac had said it was over a girl, but no one really knew. And I thought, so many people had been affected by that murder, like circles in a stream when a stone is thrown into the water. Mr O'Hara too. Ben Kincaid had been his friend.

Mysteries, I thought, as I walked down the long drive at the end of the day, *there are mysteries here*.

The lake was shrouded in smoky mist. I looked back at the statue of the college founder as he stood silently looking out over that lake. Fearfully waiting for him to move.

He didn't stir; maybe none of them ever had. But there were mysteries here, and, in spite of my fear, I wanted to find out more about them.

13

Two days later a new boy joined the class. At least new to me, though not to everybody else. Gerry Mulgrew. He looked insolent as he stood in front of Mr O'Hara. His leg was in a plaster cast covered with messages. Most of them rude.

'Mulgrew,' Aisha informed me softly. 'He likes to think he's the class bad boy. Kicked a ball at the stained-glass windows trying to break them. Couldn't even do that right. Broke his leg instead. He's actually an idiot.'

Mac leaned across the desk and whispered in her ear, 'I don't think you're allowed to call anybody an idiot any more, Aisha.' I watched wisps of her hair quiver with his breath. Was she blushing? 'It's not politically correct.'

She shrugged. 'He can take me to the Court of Human Rights.'

'I'm on your side, Aisha,' Jazz said. 'Gerry Mulgrew is an idiot.'

As if to back them up Mulgrew started heading for his desk, tripped over someone's bag and went face down on the floor.

Mr O'Hara helped him up. 'Ah, we've missed you, Mulgrew. Trying to break your other leg, are you?'

'Just lookin' for a wee bit of TLC, sir.' Mulgrew got to his feet. 'I'm still convalescing.'

Jazz laughed. 'I didn't even think you'd know what convalescing means.'

He stuck out his tongue at her, then his eyes fell on me. 'Hello, gorgeous,' he said. 'You're new. What's your name?'

Now it was my turn to blush. The class jeered and whistled. Mr O'Hara banged a book on the desk to silence them. 'Right, Mulgrew. Limp to your seat and let's get on with the lesson.'

Mulgrew winked at me and said, 'You can sign my plaster any time.' Then he made a big show of dragging his leg as he made his way past me and up the aisle. His eyes didn't leave mine and when he winked again he caused even more whistling. I turned to watch him – the whole class did – and was surprised to see him sitting in the pale-faced boy's seat.

I nudged Aisha. 'Where's the boy who usually sits there?' My eyes were scanning the class. The pale-faced boy was missing.

'There? That's always been Mulgrew's seat. Nobody else has ever sat there.'

I shook my head. 'No. No. There's been a boy sitting there since the day I started.' I pulled at Jazz's arm. 'Remember I told you he was always looking at me.'

Jazz looked blank for a moment then she smiled. 'Yeah, I remember . . . but I couldn't really see who you meant.'

'He was there. He was definitely there.' I wished I could remember his name, if I ever knew it. But his face was in front of me almost like a photograph. The intense, dark eyes, the pale face, the boy I had seen since that first day. My mouth was dry. I was trying to under-stand. Aisha touched my shoulder gently. 'You just made a mistake,' she said. 'It was probably Sam Petrie.' She pointed out the other dark-haired boy in the class, the boy who usually lay with his head on the desk. But Sam Petrie had a mop of curly hair, and a constant smile. He looked nothing like the boy I was talking about.

I was still looking all around the class. Mr O'Hara

noticed. 'Is something wrong, Tyler?'

I almost blurted it out to him. But I caught Mac looking at me, something like disapproval in his eyes. And I changed my mind. 'No, sir . . .' I muttered.

Mr O'Hara told us to open our books. The lesson began. And all I could think of was – who was the boy I had seen, day after day? Where had he gone?

He *had* been there. I couldn't be mistaken.

14

Jazz put an arm round my shoulder as we moved to the next class. 'You're in one of your dazes, Tyler Lawless. She turned to Mac, walking behind us. 'Tyler swears another boy's been sitting in Mulgrew's seat.'

'Making up more stories, eh, Tyler?' Mac's voice was full of sarcasm and it made me angry. I turned on him.

'No! I am not making up a story. I *did* see him. He *was* there. And what are you saying things like that for! What have I ever done to you?'

Mac leapt back, making out I might hit him. He held his arms in front of him for protection. 'Get crazy lady off me,' he said and he laughed. But there was no humour in the laugh.

I could have punched him then. 'I did see that boy.'

He let out a fake shocked gasp. 'Hey! A ghost. Maybe you saw a ghost.'

73

That only made me angrier. 'He wasn't a ghost. He was flesh and blood. Solid as you and me!'

Adam butted in. 'I read in a book that ghosts are like flesh and blood. You could be standing right next to one and you wouldn't know it. They look real.'

Jazz screeched with laughter. 'There must be two moons in the sky. Adam's read a book.'

They all laughed then. All except me. I was chilled to the bone. The boy with those intense, dark eyes. I could still see his face in front of me . . .

I felt Mac staring at me. 'Seems strange things are always happening to you, Tyler.' I didn't like the way he said it. But his next words floored me. 'It's not the first time you'd have seen a ghost, is it?' He put on a phoney, girlie high-pitched voice. 'I saw my teacher out doing her Christmas shopping . . . Funny since she's been dead for six months.'

Jazz stared at him. 'What are you trying to say, Mac?'

Mac tutted. 'I was playing football at her old school at the weekend. She's the talk of the place. Always making up stories like this. She was expelled from that school. They all know about her.'

'I was not expelled! I left!' My voice was too loud. Other people in the corridor turned to look at me.

Jazz swung towards me. 'You saw a ghost at your last school?'

I'd wanted things to be so different here, and now my reputation had followed me, dragged screaming to this school by Mac. He seemed to be enjoying my embarrassment. 'I think you just like to be the centre of attention, Tyler. That's what they said at your other school. You always wanted to be noticed. You caused nothing but trouble there with your stories.'

Jazz began to tell him to shut up. But a deep anger came over me. Maybe I am a little mad. Because I couldn't stop myself. I ran at him, gave him a shove that almost had him off his feet. 'Don't you *dare* say that to me!'

If I'd been a boy, I'm sure he would have punched me. 'See, that's what I mean, that's what they told me at your old school. You don't behave rationally.'

He didn't take his eyes from me. And I hated the way he looked at me. Because I had seen that look before. On so many faces. The look I thought I had left behind at my last school. The look that said . . . there was something weird about me. I was some kind of freak. 'You take that back or I'll show you just how irrational I can be!'

Jazz grabbed me or I would have rushed him again. I tried to shake her off – too roughly, it was more like a punch and I sent her sprawling against one of the statues by the wall. She tried to stop herself from falling and before I could steady myself both her and me went tumbling against the statue.

The statue moved on its plinth. Adam jumped at it, tried to hold it, so did Callum. The plinth too began to topple. Aisha grabbed at it. I saw it was hollow inside, a black hole. I wanted to crawl into it. Mac began shouting angrily at me. Aisha was yelling for someone to help her steady the plinth. Jazz jumped to her feet in a second. I was still sprawled on the ground. It must have looked as if we were having a battle royal. At least, that was the way it looked to the teacher, Mrs Craig, who came running towards us.

'Right. That's it! What on earth is happening here!' She grabbed at the statue, and with Adam and Callum's help placed it back on the plinth. Then she turned her angry eyes on the rest of us. 'You lot get to the Rector's office. We don't tolerate fighting in this school.'

She wouldn't listen to our explanations. I was willing to take all the blame, and Mac muttered that was just me trying to be the centre of attention again. No matter what I did, I couldn't seem to do anything right.

We were all marched up the corridor led by Mrs Craig, past giggling, nosy pupils, and made to sit in the chairs outside the Rector's office. The teacher left us and after knocking on the Rector's door, she stepped inside.

'I'm sorry, Jazz,' I said. 'It was an accident.'

Jazz shrugged her shoulders. 'I know. Don't worry about it.'

Mac wasn't so willing to forgive me. 'This is your fault, Tyler,' he snapped at me. 'Getting us all into trouble. Just like in your last school.'

Jazz told him to shut up. 'You were winding her up. Leave her be.'

'Intend to from now on,' Mac said.

I got to my feet and began pacing up and down the dark hallway. I was in trouble again. And I didn't even know how it had happened. St Joseph still stood there, and for a second I was tempted to look up at his face. But I wouldn't. Instead, I turned my back on him, and pretended an interest in the long line of photographs on the wall. Year after year of memories. I wished I was in one of those photographs, and not here. 1950 would have been a good year. Everyone happy.

But not 1979. The year no one smiled. Wasn't that

the year of the murder?

There was Father Michael, the priest with the sinister eyes. I recognised him now from the photograph I had seen on the internet.

I looked along the line of boys. All grim-faced.

Mac wouldn't shut up, as if he was trying to goad me into doing something else. Jazz was still berating Mac. So was Aisha. If they all didn't shut up soon, Mr Hyslop would dive from his office and grab them by the collar. We'd be in even more trouble.

Mac had hurt me, was still hurting me. But I would not let him see me cry. Concentrate on something else, I told myself. The photograph.

I saw Mr Hyslop, just a young teacher then, but still with his wild beard. He had been a mountain climber, taking the boys on expeditions, climbing Monroes. He looked the part. I was just about to look away from the photo, when I noticed Mr O'Hara, a younger Mr O'Hara, his grey hair replaced by a thick dark mop. But it was undoubtedly him. Even better looking as a boy than he was now. I peered closer, at the boy standing beside him.

I felt my mouth go dry as I looked at him. He seemed to be staring back at me, his dark eyes intense, just the way he had stared at me, day after day, from his seat at the back of the class.

I drew in my breath. I had to be wrong. This couldn't be the same boy I had seen every day. But there he was. Staring at me from the past, staring into my soul. Exactly as I had seen him, not a moment older than when this photo was taken.

There were spots in front of my eyes. My legs were like jelly. I began to crumple. I was going to faint. I let out a gasp. Jazz was on her feet in an instant. She grabbed my arm. Just as well, because I was sure I was about to collapse.

I couldn't take my eyes from that photograph. Jazz followed my gaze. 'It's him, isn't it? The boy you've been seeing in class every day?' Her finger stabbed at the photograph. 'That's Ben Kincaid.'

15

'Is that who you saw, Tyler?' Jazz had lowered me into one of the chairs, but she couldn't contain her excitement. Her long-nailed finger pointed him out again. 'That's Ben Kincaid. Are you saying that's the boy you saw in class?'

'You can't really think the boy you saw was . . . Ben Kincaid?' Aisha had that disbelieving look on her face.

What could I say? If I was Aisha, I wouldn't believe me either. I didn't answer her. Because it couldn't be true. I couldn't have seen Ben Kincaid. He'd been dead for years. And Mac was there too, looking over Aisha's shoulder, his face grim, shaking his head, and I knew he would never believe me.

'No. I didn't see him. I didn't. I didn't.' My voice was rising, on the edge of hysteria. Aisha stepped back.

'It's OK, Tyler. Calm down,' Jazz said. She dabbed at

my brow with one of her wipes. 'We believe you . . . don't we, Aisha?'

And I turned on her. 'Believe me! Believe what, Jazz? That I saw Ben Kincaid in class every day? But why should you believe that? It's crazy. What I'm saying is crazy.' My voice was rising with every word. 'I saw a dead boy sitting in class day after day. Of course I'm crazy.' Mac smirked behind her. I turned on him too. 'I just like attention, isn't that what you said, Mac? Everybody knows about me, don't they? I see dead people. I saw Ben Kincaid sitting in class every day. I must be crazy.'

His smirk disappeared. He looked angry.

Jazz didn't answer me. She was looking behind me. I swivelled round and the Rector was there. His face was stern. His beard was quivering. How much had he heard, I wondered. 'What's all this commotion about?' he yelled at us.

Mrs Craig stepped out of the office behind him. 'They've all been fighting, Mr Hyslop.'

Mac leapt in. 'No we weren't! We weren't fighting.'

Mr Hyslop turned on him. 'When I want you to speak, I'll ask you.' His eyes fell on me. 'What were you saying, Tyler, about Ben Kincaid?'

My mouth dried up. It was Aisha who rescued me. 'Tyler writes great stories, sir. She's going to write a story about this school, sir, a ghost story.'

He looked back at me, sterner than ever. 'I've had to speak to you before about this, Tyler. I don't want to have to speak to you again. I think we can do without you using us in a story. The school has a sad enough history. We want to look to the future.' His face was white, strained with anger. He took us all into his office and gave us a telling off for fighting, didn't give anyone a chance to explain anything. And he gave us a warning. My first in this school. And I thought . . . *it's all happening again*. At last he was finished with us, dismissed us all. All except me.

'I want to have a word with you, Tyler,' he said. He waited till the door was closed before he spoke again.

'Tyler, I heard the cleaners suggest you pretend you'd seen a ghost so you could wind your friends up the way they did you. But to pretend you've seen the ghost of Ben Kincaid of all people is just a step too far. I will not have it.'

This was so unfair I could have cried.

'I know your reputation from your last school,' he said, and that only made things worse. 'I don't want a repeat of any of that nonsense here. I will not allow it, Tyler.'

Everyone knew about me. I bit my lip, tried to speak, but I was too afraid I would burst into tears. So I only nodded.

16

Keep my imagination for my stories – how often had I heard all that? But here I was in the middle of a story I couldn't understand . . . it made no sense. It was so unfair.

I'd never felt so alone. There was no one I could confide in. Not my parents, or my brother, not even Jazz. Jazz loved the idea of me seeing a ghost, but did she really believe me? I didn't think so. There was no one.

My friend Annabelle phoned me that night. And I knew I could never tell her what was happening either. 'How's the new school?' she asked.

'It's good.' I was determined to sound cheery and normal and as if everything was fine. 'I've made some nice friends.'

She giggled. 'Not seen any dead teachers lately?'

It would be with me for ever, that reputation. I'd

always be known as the crazy girl who saw a dead teacher. Now a dead boy in class. I snapped at Annabelle. Didn't mean to. But I couldn't help it.

'Of course I haven't. That was all a silly mistake.'

I could hear the friendliness in her tone change. 'Keep your hair on. I was only joking.' There was a cold silence on the line for a moment. But Annabelle could never stay silent for long. 'So . . . who's the boy who was asking about you?'

Mac, she was talking about Mac. 'What boy?' I asked anyway.

'He's gorgeous . . . Asian. He was playing football at our school at the weekend. He was asking all about you.'

'And I suppose everybody took great pleasure in telling him all about me and all the crazy things I said.'

She let out a long exasperated sigh. 'I certainly didn't tell him anything.' She was going to hang up in a minute if I didn't stop talking to her like this. 'Look, some of the boys told him . . . you know what boys are like . . . but, I've been dying to ask . . . is he your boyfriend?'

'No!' I snapped at her. 'I don't even consider him a friend. He thinks I'm weird. Now he'll think I'm even weirder.'

'Oh, Tyler, I wish I could come and visit you . . . but because of this girl going missing, my mum and dad won't let me out of the house after dark.'

I would have loved in that moment to confide in her, tell her everything that had happened. Annabelle and I had been good friends once, going to sleepovers in each other's houses, whispering secrets to each other. All that had stopped when I started seeing things. Her parents had made sure of it. So how could I talk to her now? And again I realised there was no one I could tell.

'Debbie Lawson didn't go missing,' I said. 'She just ran off, didn't she?'

'On the telly tonight the police said they are beginning to think she never left the area. That something might have happened to her here in the town. They've warned everybody to be extra vigilant, young girls especially . . . that was the words they used. Extra vigilant.'

I spent a lot of time thinking after Annabelle's phone call. Mac hated me. Mr Hyslop had heard all about me too. I would soon lose Jazz and Aisha as my friends if things went on like this. But I still had the power to change things. Make it all right. And I vowed tomorrow,

I *would* make it all right. I was going to forget the boy I had seen sitting in the back of the class. I'd tell Jazz and Aisha . . . and Mac too. Especially Mac, that I had been mistaken.

And my common sense told me I probably had been. I mean, how could I have seen a dead boy? Ben Kincaid. That was too stupid to be true. No wonder no one believed me. I had kept quiet about the statues. Why hadn't I kept my mouth shut about the boy I'd seen? Well, I would keep my mouth shut from now on. I wanted friends and fun. I didn't want this.

Maybe, I thought, having an imagination like mine could drive you into madness. Into believing things that were impossible.

I wanted to prove that I wasn't mad. That I didn't want to be the centre of attention. I was going to end this.

Before I went to bed, I wrote everything that had happened down in my diary, as if it was a story I was writing. But I finished this story off. The boy never came again. He disappeared from my life. And I woke the next morning to discover it had all been a dream, a terrible nightmare.

And by the time I closed my diary, I felt so much better. Ben Kincaid was dead again.

17

I woke just after midnight. Alert immediately. I could see the time illuminated on the clock beside my bed.

12.01.

Something had awoken me. In an icy second I knew what that something was.

Someone was in the room with me.

Not just in the room. Someone was sitting at the foot of my bed.

'Mum . . . ?' my voice croaked out in a whisper. And why was I asking that? It wasn't Mum, I knew that. I tried to pull my duvet up around me and it wouldn't move. Trapped by the weight of whoever was sitting there.

Ice cold.

I was ice cold. The bed was ice cold. My feet, my hands, my whole body shivered with cold. I didn't know what to do. I lay facing the clock. 12.01. Too terrified to turn, too terrified to peer over the covers and see who was there.

And yet, somewhere inside me I knew who it was.

Him.

Ben Kincaid.

The boy with the pale face. His dark eyes always watching me. Not scary in the classroom. In daylight. But here, in midnight dark, in the black silence of my own bedroom, too terrifying to think about.

Could I hear him breathing? Did ghosts breathe? Or was that the breath of the wind outside. I longed to leap to my feet, throw the covers back, confront him. If I'd been writing this in a story, that's what I would have done.

But I was too terrified to move. And what would I see?

And why was he here? And even thinking it, I answered my own question. He knew what I had written in my diary, that I had made him disappear; I had killed him off, and he wasn't going to let me do that. He had come here to warn me. To let me know he wouldn't leave me be.

A movement, the covers grew taut. As if whoever was

sitting at the end of my bed was leaning towards me. I imagined his face coming closer.

Please, let me have the courage to look!

But there was no courage in me. I wanted to sink deep into the bed, sure I could feel his dead breath on my face.

Did I hear a voice? Was it only in my mind?

Help me, Tyler. A whispered plea. And again. *Help me, Tyler.* Words that seemed to drift like an icy breeze against my ear.

I could take it no longer. I had to get out of that bed. Had to see for myself who was there. If I thought about it a moment longer, my courage would leave me. With my eyes still closed, I threw back the duvet, I rolled from the bed, away from him, expecting at any second his cold hand to clutch at me, pull me back. I hit the wall. Curled up there for what seemed an age of time. My hands balled into fists, pressing against my eyes. Terrified to look. Imagining when I did, his face close against my own, his dead eyes staring into mine.

But I had to see. I finally had to look.

And he was gone.

The room was empty. No one here but me.

Had he ever been there? Had anyone?

Or were moments like these more signs of my madness? I scrambled ever further into the corner. I drew up my legs, hugged my knees. My eyes scanned the room. I expected something to leap out from every corner. Every shadow a threat.

There was no one here. This was my bedroom. I knew every inch of it. But I needed the light. The dark was making me too afraid. My quaking hand reached for the lamp to switch it on.

I blinked at the sudden light. My bed was crumpled, the window closed. I looked at the clock again.

12.01 . . .

The time I had first woken up . . . but that couldn't be right. Minutes, many minutes had passed since then. How could time have stood still?

Or had it all been a dream? A nightmare?

I looked all around the room, and my eyes came to rest on my keys hanging where I always put them, on a hook beside the door. They were swinging back and forth, back and forth, as if someone had just moved them. Just touched them.

I watched them all the rest of that night.

And they never stopped swinging.

18

Mum said I looked pale next morning. 'Pale as a ghost' were her exact words. They made me shiver. No wonder I was pale. I hadn't gone back to my bed. Stayed crouched in that corner. Had hardly slept all night, and when I did drop off, my head falling on my knees, my sleep had been filled with dreams – dreams of dark figures standing in the shadows of my room, long fingers reaching out to me, and whispers in the dark.

Help me, Tyler.

I would leap awake and focus my eyes on every dark recess, sure I could see something moving. I so wanted to run into Mum and Dad's room, crawl into bed between them, just as I had when I was a little girl. But I didn't even dare to move from the room, because those keys never stopped swinging, and I was sure if I opened the door someone . . . something would be there waiting for me.

'Are you feeling OK?' Mum asked once again.

I wondered if I could ask to take the day off school – but immediately decided against it. She would want me to go back to bed, tuck me in there, and I could not bear the thought of going into that room again.

I walked to school in a daze, and Aisha and Jazz caught up with me as I stood on the little arched bridge over the mist-covered lake.

'It's eerie, isn't it?' Jazz said, taking me by surprise.

'I've never even seen the other side. There's always been a mist hovering over it.'

'You're the writer,' Aisha said. 'If this was one of your stories . . . what would be on the other side?'

And I imagined another world, another dimension, another time. Nothing of this world at all.

Jazz nudged me. 'Don't look so scared. There's only trees and bushes. Nothing mysterious at all.'

'It's lovely in summer,' Aisha said. 'We go round there and have picnic lunches.'

My imagination wouldn't let me picture it in summer, in sunshine. The water was too dark. The winter bare branches hung too low, their bony fingers scratching the surface of the water menacingly.

'There isn't a body down there, if that's what you're thinking,' Jazz said, as if I'd asked her. 'Remember? The lake was dragged. Wherever Ben Kincaid's body is, it isn't down there.'

Could she read so clearly in my face what I was thinking?

'You look terrible, Tyler,' Aisha said.

I so wanted to tell them what had happened. And I wondered if I could. Tell them about the figure on my bed, the cold, the whispered words. But all I said was, 'I didn't sleep too well.'

'No wonder,' Jazz said, 'after the day you had yesterday.'

'I thought you wouldn't be talking to me,' I said. And I hadn't. I'd expected to be ignored.

Aisha smiled. 'Don't be silly. You made a mistake. It happens, and you have such an imagination.'

What she was telling me was that I hadn't seen Ben Kincaid in the classroom, I couldn't have. And surely that was what I wanted.

'Me and Aisha talked about it last night,' Jazz said. 'And we've decided we talked too much about the murder . . .'

Aisha broke in. 'We decided *you* talked too much

about the murder, Jazz.'

Jazz waved that away as if it wasn't important. 'Whatever . . .' she said. 'And then we shouldn't have wound you up about the school being haunted.'

'*You* were the one who wound her up!' Aisha said.

Jazz rolled her eyes. Her pierced eyebrow shot up. 'Anyway, your imagination did the rest. So . . . we're going to forget about it. Start afresh. What do you think?'

I wanted to tell her I had already decided that last night. Had even closed the whole affair up in my diary . . . and then . . . the cold feeling of someone sitting on my bed in the dark, the clock stopping at 12.01, the whispered words . . . *Help me, Tyler.*

I wanted to put it behind me. I wanted to start afresh. I didn't think Ben Kincaid was going to let me.

But I wasn't going to tell them that. It would do me no good at all. They were giving me the second chance I wanted. I was going to take it. Whatever happened after this, I would keep to myself.

But I knew it wasn't over.

Ben Kincaid wouldn't let it be over.

19

I had an awful day at school. Everywhere I went I had pupils laughing at me, or asking if I'd seen any more ghosts. The word had gone round the whole school I'd claimed Ben Kincaid had been sitting at the back of the class. I was a nutter. A weirdo. Mac had to be behind it. I was grateful Jazz and Aisha stayed beside me. I don't think I could have borne it if they hadn't.

The day couldn't be over quick enough; I longed to go home. Yet, as soon as I stepped inside the door of my own house, I knew there was another horror facing me. My bedroom.

I didn't dare go in it.

Jazz called me that evening. I lay stretched across the sofa, dreading the moment I'd be expected to go to bed. Couldn't bear the thought of going back into that room.

I was miserable and scared too. Was I going mad?

'I've been thinking about you all day,' she said. 'I don't think you're crazy, like everybody else does, Tyler.' She said it as if that would comfort me. 'Now don't tell Aisha I said this, because she's made me promise not to mention it again . . . but . . . I think you're psychic. Like a medium maybe.'

'No, I'm not,' I told her, because that sounded really crazy. I was an ordinary girl, and things like that didn't happen to ordinary girls. There was a reasonable explanation for everything that was happening. I was sure of it.

Me, a medium? That really was nonsense.

Jazz didn't want to listen. She'd decided I was psychic, and that was that. 'Tyler, I think we should have a seance.'

'No way!' I almost shouted it. There was no way I was taking part in anything like that.

'I don't mean we're going to sit around holding hands and chanting. But we could use the ouija board, see if we can find out what's happening. It's worth a try, isn't it?'

'This isn't a game, Jazz.' Jazz, none of them knew the half of it. I'd never told them about the statues that moved. Or . . . *Help me, Tyler . . .*

'I know it's not a game. But it might help. Help you understand. It's worth a try.'

Would it help? I didn't know what Ben Kincaid wanted of me. But I was sure he wasn't going to let me go . . . unless . . . The thought came to me. Maybe she was right. Maybe this would help. 'Have you done this before?'

'Lots of times,' she said, at once. 'It's great fun . . . and it tells you things . . . but never anything bad,' she assured me. 'I don't know how it works, but it does.'

'And you have a ouija board?'

There was a pause on the line. 'Not exactly a ouija board. I use a tumbler, and bits of paper with the alphabet written on them.' I heard myself giggle. Jazz sounded offended. 'But it works exactly the same way. And it'll be a laugh.'

Maybe that's what made me finally agree. The idea of the tumbler and Jazz's insistence that it was a channel to the other side. It made me laugh, brought the whole thing down to earth. It wouldn't do any harm. And who knows, it might even help.

Jazz was good for me, I decided.

And that night, when I did dare to go back to my room, and slip into bed, the fear somehow left me. Ben

Kincaid was getting what he wanted. We were going to have a seance. I wasn't forgetting him.

I slept peacefully all night.

At school, Mac still seemed angry at me. Though, in fact, I was the one who should have been angry at him. What had he been saying about me at my old school? What had he been asking about me, and why?

Aisha was really annoyed when Jazz told her about our night with the tumbler.

'You do this all the time, Jazz! You're not supposed to be encouraging her. You'll just get her into more trouble.'

'It's my decision,' I tried to assure her.

I'd wondered why Jazz had told her at all, if she knew she was going to be so annoyed about it. But Jazz insisted she had to tell her. 'Me and Aisha don't have secrets from each other. I just wish she'd stop moaning about it. She's worse than my old granny.'

'Well, I'm not coming,' Aisha said snappily. Her parents would never allow it, she said. 'My mum would go spare if I took part in anything like that.'

'And what do you think my mother would do, Aisha?' Jazz stood with her hands on her hips, overacting the completely shocked bit. 'My mum's a good Catholic woman. She'd kill me. That's why I'm waiting till her line-dancing night before we do it.'

Callum decided against it too. Unfortunately, Mac was up for it. I couldn't understand why. Not when he seemed to hate me so much.

'I didn't think the boys would be coming, Jazz.' The thought of Mac being there scared me. Jazz tutted. 'We'd never get the spirits to come through for just two of us, Tyler.'

Adam burst out laughing. I almost laughed too, she said it so seriously. And he was coming too, it seemed. That made me feel better. I liked Adam. Although it seemed the main reason the boys were agreeing to come was because Jazz's mum made a mean cheesecake and always had one in the fridge for Jazz's friends.

So it was settled for Thursday, the night Jazz's mum went to her line dancing. I even began to look forward to it.

But something almost stopped me getting there.

When I told my mum and dad I was going out, Dad was all against it.

'There's a police warning. Young girls shouldn't be

allowed out after dark. They're beginning to think that Debbie lassie was abducted from somewhere here in this town. Somebody reported seeing her with a man in the town after she was meant to have left.'

'Och, there's been all sorts of reports, Dad,' Mum said. 'That Debbie Lawson's like Elvis. She's been spotted everywhere.'

'Doesn't matter, they've got to follow up every lead, no matter how tenuous.'

'But I'm only going to Jazz's house. To stay in. I won't go out.' Now that it was planned I didn't want to miss it.

'Oh, let her go,' Mum insisted. 'She's made a nice friend there. And I can run her there and pick her up. She'll be in no danger.' I breathed a sigh of relief and Mum winked at me. I felt a sudden pang of guilt, because Mum wouldn't be so happy if she knew what we were planning. Getting in touch with the dead. Mum hated anything like that. I was deceiving her. I didn't want to but I had no choice.

20

'Mum's picking me up at ten o'clock,' I told Jazz when I arrived.

'Plenty of time for us to contact the dead,' Jazz whispered.

I had wondered all the way to her house if I was doing the right thing coming here. Maybe I would only be making things worse. But when Jazz said that, I laughed. The idea of summoning the spirits before ten o'clock was so ridiculous it chased all my fear away.

While the boys got stuck into the cheesecake, Jazz and I cleared and polished her dining-room table.

'It has to be really slidy so the tumbler can move quickly,' she said, very matter of factly, as if contacting the dead was something she did everyday of the week. Then she produced a whisky glass filled with squares of paper. She'd obviously been busy since she'd got in from school. Each square had a letter of the alphabet printed on it, and two other squares had the words YES and NO written on them. She put the tumbler in the middle of the table and placed the squares alphabetically in a circle around it with the YES and NO opposite each other.

Jazz dimmed the lights and lit candles and placed them all round the room. Their light flickered and reflected on the glass tumbler and cast moving shadows on the walls.

Adam's face appeared round the kitchen door, he had a tea towel wrapped round his head like a turban. 'I am the spirit of the tumbler . . . ask me anything. I am your servant.'

I giggled, because he sounded more like a dalek than a spirit.

He didn't get the chance to say another word. Jazz was taking all this much too seriously to allow that. She whipped the towel from his head and ordered him to sit down.

'This is no way to treat the spirits,' she said. 'We don't want to annoy them before we start.'

Adam made a face at me and I giggled again. Couldn't help it. This was going to be fun, nothing scary about it at all. Adam and Mac wouldn't let that happen.

I knew from the way they sneaked a glance at each other that they intended to have a laugh about the whole thing.

At the start, it was hard to take it seriously.

The bits of paper would blow off the table every time a door opened, and the candles kept going out.

But, by the time we all took our places, and the house was silent, and candlelight illuminated our faces, it didn't seem so funny then. I'd never done anything like this before. Maybe we were tempting fate even trying it. My feelings must have shown on my face. Adam leaned towards me. He whispered, 'Don't look so worried, Tyler. You don't really think we're going to contact the dead through this?'

Mac just stared at me. I knew what he was thinking. That I would take over the whole thing, try to get all the attention he thought I craved.

'OK, fingers on the glass,' Jazz said, and we all laid our index fingers lightly on top of the tumbler.

'Spirit of the tumbler . . . are you there?'

The glass shot to the square that said YES.

Jazz immediately took her fingers off the glass and yelled at Adam, 'You pushed that!'

He grinned. 'No? It must have been the spirits.

Honest!' Then he laughed and half the squares blew off the table again. It took ages to pick them all up and place them back where they'd been.

'For goodness' sake,' Jazz said. 'We've only got till ten o'clock!'

Adam laughed again. 'Spirits got to be back in their graves for then, eh?' He laughed so much the rest of the paper fluttered off the table.

'Och, this is a waste of time,' Mac said. 'Let's have more cheesecake.'

But Jazz insisted. 'It'll work. You wait and see. You can laugh all you want, but it's going to work.'

So again, once everything was back in order, and Jazz had threatened the boys with no more cheesecake if they didn't behave, we put our fingers on the glass and Jazz closed her eyes and whispered, 'Are the spirits with us?'

For a moment nothing happened. I was almost ready to giggle again. And then . . . the tumbler moved. I pulled my finger away, looked at Adam. 'Is that you again?'

He shrugged. 'Not this time, I promise.' And I knew from the baffled look on his face that he wasn't lying.

'Tyler,' Jazz said. 'Put your finger back on the glass. The spirit is here.' She closed her eyes again and said softly, in a voice that didn't sound like Jazz at all, 'Have you a message for someone in this room?'

As soon as my finger touched the tumbler, it moved again. First to the letter T and then to the letter Y.

I pulled my finger away so quickly the glass trembled on the table. 'It's going to spell out my name.' I looked around, at Jazz, at Adam and at Mac. 'One of you is pushing it.' I kept my eyes on Mac. I wanted him to admit that it was him.

'Hey, yours is the last name I would spell out.'

'Put your finger back, Tyler,' Jazz said. And I did. She drew in a deep breath. 'Have you a message for Tyler?'

The glass immediately slid to YES.

'What is your message?' Jazz was really into it now. Her words almost came out like a chant.

The tumbler moved again. First to the letter H, then around the circle to E and then L. Slowly at first, then faster and faster. I saw Mac's finger flying off it moved so fast, yet still it flew around the table. And Adam's finger slipped off too. They weren't pushing it. And neither was I. What was happening? P . . . to M . . . to E . . .

'Help me,' Jazz said. 'It's asking you to "help me".'

The glass was still moving faster and faster round the table, spelling out its message again. And then again.

HELP ME, TYLER.

I remembered the words I had heard in my head, surely only in my head, the night the clock stopped – the night he had visited me in my room. *Help me, Tyler*, he had whispered.

'But who are you?' I shouted as if it could hear me. And I knew the answer even before the glass began to move again. I knew the name it would spell out. B . . . E . . . N.

'Ben Kincaid.' Jazz's voice seemed to come from far away. I couldn't take my eyes off that glass. Faster and faster it raced round the table, touching the K, then the I, flying to the square marked N. Then round the table and almost sending the square marked C fluttering to the floor. Jazz's finger fell from the tumbler, then Mac's, until the only finger on it was my own. Then even I couldn't hold it. It flew over the edge and smashed to the ground on Jazz's tiled dining-room floor.

HELP ME, TYLER.

A plea from Ben Kincaid from beyond the grave.

But how could I possibly help him? He was dead!

21

Mac still thought I'd pushed it. 'Funny your finger was the only one left on the glass,' he said afterwards.

'I didn't push it!' I yelled it at him, wishing he could understand how scared I was. Jazz understood. She seemed to be revelling in the whole thing.

'Why would she push it?' Jazz asked him.

'Maybe she wants to be famous for five minutes. Or in her case a little longer. She did the same in her last school. Telling people she saw a dead teacher. Making things up.' He spat the words out as if they disgusted him.

'That's why I think Tyler is a psychic,' Jazz insisted. 'This has happened to her before.'

Mac turned away in disgust. 'Aw come on, Jazz.'

Jazz pulled him round to face her again. 'You know she didn't push that tumbler, Mac. You saw her face . . .

look at her face now.'

Mac did, stared at me, and then looked away quickly. 'She's a good actress.'

I'd had enough of him. 'Stop talking about me as if I'm not here. I didn't push that glass. I don't understand what's happening either.'

But I'd never convince Mac.

Jazz pushed him and Adam into the kitchen for more cheesecake. Then she sat me down on the sofa and said very seriously, 'I think I've figured out how Ben Kincaid wants you to help him.' She spoke as if she was an expert in the paranormal. 'He needs you to help him get to the other side.'

I heard a spluttered giggle from the kitchen. The boys at the kitchen door, mouths full of cheesecake, obviously listening.

'The other side of what?' I asked her.

'He's trapped here, in this world. He can't move on. Something's keeping him here and he needs you to help him.'

'So what's keeping him here . . . and why does it have to be me?'

Jazz shrugged. 'Because you're psychic. You came to the school and you're psychic. He's never been able to get through to anyone before, but he can get through to you. And he'll let you know how to help him.'

But I didn't want him to let me know. The thought of it freaked me out. Yet, in a way, she was right. Ben Kincaid wasn't going to let me go.

Dad picked me up bang on ten o'clock. 'Have a nice time?' he asked.

I nodded. But I hadn't had a nice time. I was scared. How was I supposed to help a dead boy get to the other side?

'I'm so glad I wasn't there,' Aisha said next morning. She was waiting for me at the school gate. I was glad of her company, didn't fancy walking up the long drive past the lake on my own this morning. 'Jazz phoned me. Told me all about it.'

'I don't believe any of it,' I said, wanting it to be true.

'Neither do I. One of the boys was pushing it, don't worry about it.' She squeezed my arm. 'Jazz loves things like this, she'll just wind you up. That's why I didn't want her to do it.'

It made me feel better, for a while anyway.

The bell rang, and I began to hurry towards the classroom. Aisha was held back by Callum, but I moved on ahead of the others, none of them in any hurry to get to our class. Mac was holding forth about something. I nudged past him. I was first into the classroom . . . or I thought I was. I stepped in, and there, sitting in the seat at the back where I had always seen him, was the boy with the pale face, the dark eyes.

Ben Kincaid.

I leapt back out, stumbling into Mac, and Callum and Adam. 'He's there,' I said, breathless. I clutched at Callum's jacket. 'Ben Kincaid. He's sitting at the back.'

'I don't believe you,' Mac said, pushing me aside. Jazz was right with him.

'It's him,' I said.

They stepped into the classroom. *Please let them see him*, I prayed. *Please let them say they see him.*

Mac turned back to me. He took a deep breath. 'She's right. He's there,' he said.

At last, I thought, *someone else sees what I can see.* And I was so glad that someone was Mac. Then his hand encircled my arm and he pulled me gently towards him, into the classroom. I didn't want to look again, but I had to.

'There you go,' Mac said. 'Ben Kincaid. Large as life.'

I could hardly bear to open my eyes. I only peered through my lashes. I saw the dark hair, the same pale face, the boy sitting at the back of the class watching me.

'It's him,' I mumbled. And I turned away again.

They all crowded into the doorway behind me. There was a cold silence. I felt Jazz touch my arm gently. 'Tyler . . . look again.'

I dared another look. My eyes wide this time. The boy sitting at the back of the class stared back. He called out. 'What are you lot staring at?' His voice was cheeky. I saw then (how could I not have noticed it before?) his hair was not so dark, his face was not so pale. It was Sam Petrie.

He definitely wasn't Ben Kincaid.

'But I thought . . . I was sure . . .' How could I have made such a stupid mistake?

Mac smirked. 'Told you it would work,' he said to no one in particular.

And I realised then he'd been responsible. He'd held the others back deliberately. He'd made sure Sam Petrie was sitting in that seat, made sure that I would be the first into the class. He wanted to trick me . . . and it had worked.

I hated him.

22

I'd blown it. I knew that as soon as I realised that the boy wasn't Ben Kincaid. I had mistaken Sam Petrie for him. Now they thought I'd been mistaken all along. Or lying. Mac's eyes told me that was exactly what he believed. I had made the whole thing up. He had proved it. 'How could you be so rotten?' I asked him.

He shrugged. 'Isn't it better to know you were wrong . . . or would you rather it had been a ghost?'

'It's an easy mistake to make.' Aisha tried to make me feel better. 'Sam does look a bit like that photo of Ben Kincaid outside Mr Hyslop's office.'

'Sam Petrie doesn't look a bit like that.' Mac spat the words out, and though I hated to say it, he was right. Sam Petrie didn't look at all like Ben Kincaid. But just for a second, when I had first peeked into the classroom, there had been a momentary resemblance.

'I know what's happened,' Callum said. And we all listened, as if he really was the cleverest boy in the school. 'Tyler, when you were outside the Rector's office that first day . . . did you look at the photographs on the wall?'

I tried to remember exactly what I'd seen that day. I had stood up and turned to the wall . . . and, yes, there had been the photograph where no one was smiling. 1979. The one with Father Michael in it and . . . of course Ben Kincaid must have been there too, though I hadn't noticed him then. At least, I thought I hadn't. I nodded.

'Well, that's it. You've seen the photo of Ben Kincaid. You come into the class and see wee Sam there. There's a passing resemblance. Your subconscious gets the two of them mixed up. Genuine mistake.'

Adam grinned. 'Hey, listen to Clement Freud here.'

Callum corrected him. 'It's Sigmund Freud actually. *He* was the famous psychiatrist.'

Mac looked disgusted. 'Seems Tyler makes a lot of genuine mistakes. A dead teacher in a supermarket queue, a dead boy sitting in the class. Come on!'

I was angry, but I had no answer to that. Jazz was the only one who seemed to believe me. She wanted desperately for it to be true because she loved ghost stories. Jazz spoke up for me. 'I think she did see Ben Kincaid. He appeared to her in class. He came through to her at our seance. He needs her to help him.' She put her arm round my shoulder. 'And we're going to find out how.'

She was so enjoying the idea of some strange haunting going on. Why couldn't it all be happening to Jazz? I bet she wouldn't be afraid.

But the dreary days passed and nothing else happened. I moved in a dream – a nightmare. I felt sick to my stomach. I walked home every day down the long drive, past the misty lake, past the shops with the newspaper headlines that were all about the missing girl.

COME BACK DEBBIE

And I wondered if anyone at school would want me back if I went missing.

It was our Steven who cheered me up. He passed his driving test, first attempt (we'd never hear the end of that) and he insisted on taking the whole family out for a drive in the car.

'I tell you what,' Dad said, 'you can take us to that little country pub we like. I'll treat us all to a meal, and I can have a beer for a change.'

'And for once, it won't be Mum's taxi service. When me and Dad or Tyler go out, Steven can pick us all up,' Mum said.

Steven didn't look too happy about that, but he was desperate to show off his driving skills. Skills might be a bit of an exaggeration. Almost running us into a ditch. Crashing the gears as he went up a hill. And swerving so hard to avoid some daft pheasant standing in the middle of the road he almost had us wrapped round a tree.

'How did you ever manage to pass?' I asked him after he'd stalled the car for the third time.

'He must have put a spell on the examiner,' Dad said.

But that night out was just what I needed to take my mind off things. Lift me out of that sombre mood. Mum noticed it too.

'You've been so withdrawn lately. I've been worried about you,' she said, as we waited for our meal at the pub, and Dad and Steven had a game of snooker. 'It's so good to see you smile again.'

That night I convinced myself it had been Sam Petrie I had seen all along. A boy who looked like Ben Kincaid.

The statues in the school hadn't moved at all – that had been a trick of the light . . . And the message from the tumbler (I mean, a message from a tumbler! How could I ever take that seriously?) Adam or Mac had been pushing it, of course. And that night in my bedroom? I hadn't seen anything, had I? It had all been imagination or a dream.

Everything had a logical explanation.

And treating it like that seemed to work.

Next day at school, Jazz and Aisha and I had a great time playing netball, and when I told them all about Steven's erratic driving even Mac managed a smile.

I wanted it to stay like this.

It *would* stay like this. I promised myself it would.

But there are some promises you can't keep. Some things you can't stop. And some things you cannot foresee.

23

It was Friday. I was so looking forward to the weekend. Jazz and I were going to the movies tonight. And then we were having a sleepover, my first sleepover with Jazz, at her house. Aisha said she had other plans.

'Something's going on there,' Jazz insisted. 'Aisha miss a sleepover? I think she's got a date with Mac.'

'Mac? Who would go out with that miserable so-and-so?'

Aisha was far too nice for him, that's what I was thinking as I hurried to the toilets. Mr O'Hara had excused me, told me to hurry back. The toilets were practically across the corridor from the classroom. I would only be gone for a few minutes.

It was a dark, dismal Friday. The clouds hung low outside the high windows. But I didn't feel dismal, not that day. All that was on my mind was the weekend ahead.

If I hadn't needed to go to the toilet, if I'd stayed in the classroom, it wouldn't have happened . . . would it?

Or are there things that are meant to be – going to happen no matter what you do?

I was coming out of the girls' toilets when I heard it. A soft, low chanting, rhythmic, almost peaceful. It seemed to weave its way down the gloomy passageways towards me.

I stopped and listened. At first, I thought it was the school choir practising. Not quite singing, and yet more musical than anything I'd ever heard before.

It was a prayer, some ancient, Latin prayer, winding its way towards me from somewhere in the distance. I couldn't move, though I knew I should hurry back to class. I was only steps from the classroom door, could hear Mr O'Hara's voice. Better to ignore that chant, I told myself. But I couldn't stop listening. The chant was so beautiful, so soothing and hypnotic.

I couldn't stop myself. Instead of heading back to my class, so close that I could almost reach out and touch the door handle, I turned and followed the sound.

I wasn't afraid. What was there to be afraid of from anything so beautiful?

The school was so silent. I heard a teacher shout

angrily from one of the classrooms, heard my feet tapping on the tiled floor. But otherwise there was no other sound. Just that chanting prayer. So musical, and yet not quite music.

This was no school choir, no choir of young voices either. I could imagine row upon row of black-clad monks, their hoods covering their faces, their hands locked in prayer, murmuring that beautiful prayer.

There was a statue against the wall. I looked up, and his face was turned towards the sound of the chanting too. Surely, he had always had his head bent in prayer?

Still I couldn't stop following the sound.

I turned a corner and could hear the words more clearly. I still couldn't understand them. *Depra* . . . something. It wasn't English, that much I did know.

Depra . . . a language I didn't understand – *foondis* . . . Latin probably. The only words I could make out – *Depra foondis* – they were repeated like a litany, but I still couldn't understand them.

Another corner, and here was another statue, looking towards the sound, as if his alabaster ears could hear it as clearly as mine. I was in a part of the school I had never been to before. Facing me, at the end of the corridor, was the heavy wooden door of the old chapel. The chanting was coming from behind that door. The place where Ben Kincaid was murdered. It was never used now. Not since that dreadful night. So who was in there? Who was praying in there?

I halted at the richly carved oak door. I placed my hand around the ornate brass door handle so cold to my touch, and I knew I shouldn't enter now. It would be locked. It should be locked. Ben Kincaid had died here. This was the last place I should want to go into. I should, instead, run back to my classroom. Clamp my hands over my ears to blot out that sound. It was luring me in, like a siren song, hypnotising me, and I was powerless to ignore it.

It was too late for me to run.

Slowly, I turned the handle of the door.

24

The chanting ceased as soon as the door was opened. As if the sound had suddenly been switched off. Yet, still I stepped inside. The air was chill, but I told myself it was a stone chapel, stone walls, stone floors, always cold as death. I could see my breath form like mist in the icy air.

There was no choir of monks. The chapel was empty, and dark. No candles sat in the candle-holders. And a single statue dominated the room. St Anthony. I wondered why he hadn't been moved. Patron saint of the college. It struck me then that there was no statue of him anywhere in the school. I would have thought he deserved a special place, a more public place. Not here. Alone.

But he had been witness to a murder.

What horrors must he have seen that night? I shivered. It was as if I had stepped into a refrigerator. Freezing cold. Did that mean something? That there was some presence here?

Ben Kincaid?

My heart began to pound. I wanted to turn and run, but I couldn't move.

The chapel is empty – I kept telling myself that over and over. My eyes scanned every dark alcove, every shadowy corner. *The chapel is empty.*

And behind me the door slammed shut.

I swivelled round. The door was tight shut. I pulled at the handle, and pulled. It wouldn't turn, as if it hadn't been turned for years. Stiff with age. I began to panic. The chapel was so dark. Shadows everywhere.

And then there was a movement. One of those shadows seemed to come alive. A shadow, dressed in black, kneeling in prayer at one of the small altars in the chapel. In one long movement he got to his feet. My teeth were chattering. I was desperate to run, why couldn't I move?

The figure turned. I saw his face. His long, solemn face, and his eyes, so blue they seemed to illuminate the room.

Those eyes homed in on me. I had seen them before. In a photograph, on a wall, on a computer screen.

Father Michael.

The murderer.

I was looking into the eyes of a murderer.

And then he stretched out his hand and took a step towards me.

Did I scream? I don't know if I did. I could hear a scream, but whether it was in my head or outside my head I couldn't tell. I had to get away – that was my only thought.

I pulled at the door, and still it would not open. I looked behind me, and there he was, moving closer. This time I screamed. I was certain I screamed.

And now at last the door flew open. I almost fell back, but I managed to keep my feet. I was through it in an instant. I ran from the chapel, tripped and tumbled to the ground. I rolled, looked back, saw a shadow closing in, and I screamed again.

Still no one came running out of classrooms, and I couldn't understand why. Was I still only screaming inside? I staggered to my feet and began running again. Expecting that at any second I would feel his cold hand on me, that he was floating behind me, above me, closer and closer. I dared not stop.

Help me, Tyler.

The words whispered themselves again in my ear as I

ran. From somewhere beside me. As if someone was there at my shoulder. As if Ben Kincaid was running with me. Running from his killer.

But how was I supposed to help? Ben Kincaid was dead, beyond help.

And now Father Michael had come back.

That was the really scary thing. Why had he come back?

Had the seance brought him here? Had he come back to stop me from helping Ben?

Fingers touched my shoulder. I slammed against the wall. If I could have found my voice, I would have screamed then.

'Shouldn't you be in class, Tyler?'

I jumped in fright. It was the Rector. I glanced behind him, all around the corridor. It was empty. Just him and I. He followed my gaze. 'Is something wrong?'

He already thought I was trouble. Telling him what I had just seen and heard would only sink me deeper.

I stared at him. It was the Rector who spoke to me. 'What were you doing near the chapel, Tyler?'

I felt a rush of fear. 'I . . . I thought I heard something, sir.'

He cocked his head, reminding me of a bird. 'Heard something, from the chapel? It's been closed up since . . .' He couldn't bring himself to say the words 'since the murder'. 'For years, Tyler. You could have heard nothing from the chapel.'

'I heard chanting, sir . . . I thought it was coming from in there, but . . .'

He broke in, wouldn't let me say more. 'Is this another of your – fictional! – ghost stories, Tyler?' I could almost see the capital F. He made Fictional sound like a swear word.

'I thought . . . I thought . . .' I didn't know what to say.

'I warned you I didn't want to hear any more of your stories.' His eyes, his tone, let me know he thought I was lying. I must have looked mad, staring at him, saying nothing. But what could I say? What was happening to me?

He reached out his hand and touched my arm. His voice was more gentle. 'I'm worried about you, Tyler. I can't keep putting aside the reports from your last school . . .'

I blurted out, 'That was all a mistake.'

'I will try to believe that. I'm prepared to give you another chance.' He hesitated. 'We do have a school counsellor, Tyler. Perhaps you should have a talk with her.'

The idea of that petrified me. She would think I was crazy and the horrible part was that I was beginning to think it too. Had I really heard that hypnotic chanting? Had I actually seen Father Michael?

I spoke and tried to make my voice sound normal. 'I probably heard someone playing music in one of the classrooms . . . That's what I heard. And I got lost, sir.' I laughed. Did my laugh border on the hysterical? 'Still can't find my way round this school. I should get back to my class.'

I could feel his eyes on me as I hurried back to my class. I had a feeling he was going to be watching me from now on.

25

It was midnight before I told Jazz what had happened, and we were tucked up in her pink and black bedroom (only Jazz would have a black bedroom) and Jazz was desperate to tell ghost stories. 'The midnight hour,' she said. 'The perfect time for ghost stories.' Well, I had one of my own, didn't I? A real-life ghost story.

I was glad at least she'd stopped talking about Aisha. She'd spent most of the evening wondering exactly where she could be.

'Missing a sleepover?' she kept saying. 'It has to be a boy.'

But which boy? That was what was bothering Jazz. We'd almost been thrown out of the cinema she'd talked so much about it. Halfway through the movie she took out her mobile phone and called Mac. 'Bet he's with her,' she said.

I tried to stop her, but Jazz is like a ten ton truck with the brakes not working when she gets started. Mac didn't answer and that seemed to reinforce her opinion that the two of them were together. Everyone around us started complaining, and one of the ushers stormed over and ordered her to switch the phone off or we would be asked to leave the premises. He didn't put it quite as politely as that, however. In fact, I suggested he was the one who should be asked to leave the premises, using the kind of language he had. Jazz had giggled about it all the way back to her house. I couldn't giggle. Just wasn't in the mood for it. And Jazz knew it. If she asked me once, she asked a hundred times . . . 'What's wrong with you? Something else has happened, hasn't it?' She drew up her legs and hugged her knees. She was all ears. 'I knew when you came back to class today something had happened. You were chalk white and shaking. And you've been so quiet all night. What happened, Tyler?'

And I burst into tears. Didn't want to. I was scared, that was my only excuse.

Jazz leapt from her bed and rushed to my side. She put her arms round me. And that only made me cry some more. 'Come on, what happened today?'

And in a faltering voice, stumbling over the words, I

began to tell her. Tell her about standing outside the classroom and hearing that haunting sound winding towards me.

'It was beautiful, Jazz, but I couldn't understand what they were chanting, some kind of hymn I think.'

'What hymn . . . maybe I know it. Maybe it's the key to something.'

I shook my head. 'I didn't understand it. It wasn't in English. Maybe it was Latin?'

'Well, I'm a Catholic. I might know the Latin. So what was it? Could you make out anything?'

I tried to remember. Those moments when I stopped and listened, how that sound had drawn me step by step closer to the chapel. '*Depra* . . . something . . . *foondis* . . . *depra* . . . *foondis*?' I shook my head again. 'I don't know, Jazz.'

'*Depra foondis*? It's at times like this I wish I wasn't a lapsed Catholic,' she muttered. 'But I'll ask my mum . . . or my gran, yeah, Gran. She goes to Mass every day, to make up for me I think . . . She's bound to know what it means.'

She moved in closer, eager for more. 'Go on,' she said.

So I told her. About the moment I opened the chapel

130

door, and how the singing suddenly stopped. 'There was no one there,' I said. 'The chapel was empty, at least, I thought it was and then, there in the shadows, I saw him. Father Michael.'

Jazz fell off my bed when I said that. It took her a moment to recover. 'You saw Father Michael? Wow! This is way better than any made-up ghost story.'

'Don't laugh about it, Jazz,' I said as she climbed back on the bed beside me. 'I'm so frightened and mixed up. I ran from there, I was screaming, I'm sure I was, I can't understand why the whole school didn't hear me . . . and then I felt a hand on my shoulder.'

Jazz almost fell off the bed again. 'Father Michael.'

'No. The Rector, and he seemed to be so angry with me. I didn't tell him anything about Father Michael, of course. He already thinks I'm making up ghost stories. And he knows all about what happened at my old school. Now he really does think I'm a troublemaker . . . or just crazy. He gave me a real telling off and he suggested I see the school counsellor.' I began to cry again. 'What's happening to me, Jazz? You don't think I'm crazy, do you? You believe me.'

It took her only a second to answer me, but a long second too long.

'Of course I do.'

Now it was my turn to ask. 'What's wrong?'

She seemed to be making up her mind what to tell me. It seemed an age, before she spoke. 'You went to the chapel . . . ?'

'I told you I did.'

'You followed the chanting . . . you walked to the chapel? You went inside?'

'Yes,' I said.

'Tyler, you were only out of the classroom for a few minutes. You couldn't have done all that. The chapel is at the other end of the school.'

26

I couldn't explain to Jazz how that had happened. So I couldn't prove to her I was really at the chapel. I wished I could tell her to ask Mr Hyslop, but he was one person I could never expect to back me up. And I knew Jazz wasn't lying. I'd been gone from the classroom for only a few minutes . . . and yet I had been on a journey that should have taken much, much longer. I knew she wanted to believe me, that she was looking for reasons for it happening. Where had the time gone? And I remembered the clock in my room, freezing at 12.01. Time had stood still.

Time, time, time . . . it was all to do with time. I was sure of it. If only I understood what it all meant.

At home next day, it was all I could think about.

Dad was sitting in the living room, watching the afternoon racing, when I walked in. I said nothing, just sat on the sofa across from him.

'Something wrong, Tyler?'

'Yes, something's wrong,' I wanted to say, but how could I explain all this to him?

He took his eyes off the television screen. 'Did something happen last night at Jasmine's house?'

'No, Dad,' I said. 'Jazz is great.'

'So . . . what is it?'

I shrugged. 'I wish I didn't have to go back to that school, Dad.' Best say it right out, I thought. 'I'm not happy there.'

He closed his eyes, despair written all over his face. 'Oh, Tyler, not again.'

I could get my dad to do anything for me . . . but not this.

'Dad, please listen . . .'

But he didn't let me finish. 'You've made friends there, Tyler, and the first few weeks at a new school are always difficult. You've just got to give these things time.' He touched my face. 'You've not said you've seen any . . .' He didn't want to say the words . . . dead teachers. And I didn't want him to think it. So I shook my head quickly.

'Nothing like that, Dad. I'm just not happy there,' I said.

'Give it time, please.' He tried to keep the smile on his

face, but it was a strain. 'You don't want to get a reputation for jumping from one school to another, eh?'

And I knew then I would never speak of it again. I nodded and left him to his racing, and went and sat in the kitchen.

He was right, of course. I had made friends there. And maybe it would make no difference if I left St Anthony's. Ben Kincaid would never let me go. He'd follow me home, he'd haunt my dreams, sleeping and awake, I'd never get away from him. He could reach me anywhere, travel through time and space and solid walls, and there was nowhere I could hide from him.

I dreaded going into the school on Monday, because I knew it wasn't over. I had come to the conclusion . . . the realisation . . . the acceptance, that I couldn't stop what was happening to me, and Jazz and Aisha were only still my friends because that's what friends did, stick by you through good times and bad.

They were waiting for me at the entrance door when I got to school, and they had a plan.

'We are not going to leave your side,' Aisha said. 'Jazz told me what happened.'

'If you even have to go to the girls' toilets, one of us

goes with you. No matter where you go in this school, one of us goes with you. Then nothing can happen to you . . . if we're there.'

'And if it does,' Aisha assured me, 'then we'll be your witnesses.'

I was touched by their concern. And I was glad. Because I never wanted to be alone here anyway.

For a day or two things settled down. I became used to the boy at the back of the class. Gerry Mulgrew. He did seem to fancy me. He was always grinning at me and winking.

And to cheeky little Sam Petrie with his mop of dark hair. He didn't look a bit like Ben Kincaid. Not now that I saw him every day. His face was not so pale, his eyes not so striking. He'd stopped sleeping on the desk, and now he was always smiling.

And true to their word. Jazz and Aisha never left my side.

And when they were with me, statues never moved. There was no sign of Father Michael or Ben Kincaid. I was safe – and after those first days I began to relax. I even began to believe maybe it *was* all over. That I had been wrong. Maybe in some unknown way I had already helped Ben Kincaid . . . he had already passed to the other side.

And then Jazz suggested we go back to the chapel.

27

I thought Jazz was mad for suggesting it, but she had a reason.

'You say you were lured there, by that chanting. Well, maybe Ben Kincaid lured you there for a reason. He was murdered there, Tyler. Maybe that's where he's trapped. We'll be there with you. We won't leave you. I mean, I'm scared even thinking about it, but I think we should go.'

Aisha agreed. 'You'll see it's just an ordinary place. Just a drab old room. It doesn't even feel holy any more.'

I was puzzled. 'You've been in there? But it's locked. Mr Hyslop says it's always locked.'

Jazz grinned. 'You remember talking to Mrs Sorenson? She let us go in there once.'

The cleaner who worked on that floor. Yes, I remembered Mrs Sorenson.

'She just happens to be a real good friend of my mum,

and she's got a key to the chapel. She's the one who goes in and cleans it up now and again.'

'And she'll give you the key?'

'Let's just say she'll lend it to me . . . but she won't know she has.'

Aisha rolled her eyes. 'You mean you're going to pinch it.'

'Borrow it, Aisha,' Jazz said. 'There's a difference.'

We went during lunchbreak the next day. It took us ages to walk there. Jazz was right, I couldn't have made it there and back in just a few minutes. We seemed to turn corner after corner, past statues in alcoves, statues set against walls. Aisha noticed me watching them as we walked. 'Do they give you the creeps?'

She wasn't Catholic; maybe she would understand. 'A bit,' I said.

Aisha smiled. 'I like them. They're nothing to be scared of, Tyler. They're only plaster and paint.'

'I know,' I said, as if I believed her.

At last we reached the chapel. I felt my mouth dry up.

I stared at the carved oak door. 'I don't think I want to go in there.'

'You don't think Father Michael will be there, do you?' Aisha asked.

'Or a choir of monks, still chanting?' Jazz nudged me and winked. She put the key into the lock and turned it.

I reached out my hand. The brass handle was cold to the touch, ice cold. The door was heavy, it took all three of us to push it open . . . yet it had slipped open easily for me.

What would I find in here? My heart was hammering in my chest and I was biting my lip, almost too afraid to look.

And there was nothing.

No atmosphere, no feeling of menace, the rows of the choir were empty. The pews bare. The statue of St Anthony still silently dominated the chapel. I looked at the altar where I could have sworn I had seen Father Michael kneeling in prayer.

Jazz squeezed my shoulder. 'Well?'

I didn't answer for a moment. I *had* been here before, I wanted to tell them, but I decided against it.

I shook my head. 'There's nothing. It's just an old chapel.'

Saying that made me feel better. It *was* just an old chapel. So why had I been drawn here? Because Ben Kincaid had died here . . . ? Because he needed my help?

'I've been thinking,' Jazz said. 'Maybe Ben Kincaid

needs you to pray for him here. This is where he died. Maybe that's why you saw Father Michael here too. He can't move on either, because of the terrible thing he did.'

Jazz, it seemed, had it all worked out.

'St Anthony's the patron saint of lost things, did you know that?' Jazz asked.

I didn't know that. She went on. 'Ben Kincaid's lost, lost between this life and the next. Maybe that's why you were brought here. To the statue of St Anthony. So he can find Ben and help him move on.'

Maybe that was true, I thought, there had to be a reason why I'd been brought here. 'I'd like to light a candle.' I seemed to be whispering it to myself.

Jazz smiled. Pulled a candle from her pocket. 'See, I already thought of that.'

The only candlestand was at the foot of the statue of St Anthony. I dared a look at the kindly plaster face. He was watching me. Had he always been watching over me, I wondered.

'How are we going to light it?' Aisha asked.

'I brought a box of matches.' Jazz produced it from her pocket.

She pushed the box at me.

My hand was shaking as I lit the candle, and Jazz and

Aisha stepped back as if this was my moment, only mine. 'What do I say?' I asked Jazz.

She shrugged her shoulders, 'Say a prayer for Ben Kincaid. Maybe that's all he needs.'

I held the candle in both hands, and looked up again at the face of St Anthony. The flickering light seemed to make his eyes come alive, gave his face the warmth of life. *Please give Ben Kincaid peace*, I said silently. *If he's trapped here, help him move on*. I didn't add, at least not consciously, that I wanted nothing more to do with it. I too wanted peace.

I felt better as we pulled the door of the chapel closed and Jazz locked it again. I had left it in St Anthony's hands. Maybe now Ben Kincaid would have someone more powerful than me to help him.

But Mac was doing his best still to annoy me. I hoped Aisha wasn't stuck on him. He didn't deserve her. He didn't deserve anybody.

We were in the school cafe at lunchtime, and Jazz had told the boys that she and Aisha had been with me for two days and nothing had happened.

He tapped his chin thoughtfully and stared at me. 'Funny that, eh? Nothing happens except when you're on your own. Isn't that strange?'

I'd had enough of Mac. I leapt at him. 'Why is it so hard for you to believe me? What have I ever done to you!'

It was Callum who stuck up for me. 'Leave her be, Mac.'

Mac stepped away from the table. His eyes didn't leave me. 'You know what I think? You all pussyfoot around her – you, Aisha, 'cause you're too nice to offend her, and you, Jazz, because you love ghost stories. What you should be doing is telling her she's talking rubbish. Talk some sense into her. She's making a fool of you both.'

Did he always mean to hurt me so much? And why did I let him?

But I wouldn't let Mac spoil my mood. I had Jazz and Aisha, and I didn't need his approval.

Even when Jazz came in the next day with her granny's prayer book and told me she'd found out what the chanting I had heard meant, it didn't bother me. It was as if that had happened to someone else.

She flicked through the well-worn pages of the old missal until she found the page she wanted.

'*De profundis* . . . that's what you heard.'

I shrugged. 'If you say so.'

'Look there.' She pointed triumphantly.

De Profundis

The Prayer for the Dead

De profundis clamavi ad te, Domine
Domine, exaudi vocem meam.

And on the opposite page the translation.

Out of the depths I have cried to Thee,
O Lord,
Lord, hear my voice.

Out of the depths . . .

Once again I could hear words chant in my head. So clear now. *De profundis clamavi ad te* . . .

But I shook the memory away. 'Doesn't matter what it means, Jazz,' I said, remembering I had passed the responsibility on to someone else. 'Because it's over. Nothing is ever going to happen again. It's over.'

But something did happen.

28

It was halfway through the afternoon. The bell had rung and we were hurrying from one class to another, the three of us, laughing. The corridor was buzzing with people, classes on the move, pupils bustling against each other.

I stepped ahead of Jazz and Aisha to avoid a crush. 'Come on, you two!' I turned back and called to hurry them on. And when I swung round again, there he was. Standing right in front of me.

Ben Kincaid.

Couldn't miss the dark hair, the deep-set eyes. So close I could have kissed him. His face, his form as solid as my own.

Things like this were only supposed to happen when you're alone. In the dark. With shadows all around you. Not on a bright day, in a noisy corridor surrounded by other people.

For a second I couldn't breathe. As if I'd forgotten how. I stared at him, and then turned back towards Jazz and Aisha again, for they must be able to see him too. But though I could still see them, it was as if they were lost in some kind of dream world. The buzz in the corridor was muted. My friends were moving towards me as if they were in slow motion, yet never getting any closer. I could hear their voices, drawn out as if the sound too were in slow motion. As if time itself was being slowed down.

I turned to look ahead down the corridor and he was still there, so close. And behind him, the statue of St Teresa. Her hands seemed to be reaching down to him; the flowers clutched in her fingers were almost touching his black hair.

'What do you want?' I yelled at him, expecting Jazz or Aisha to hear me, for everyone to hear me, but no one did. 'Leave me alone!' My voice was a scream.

His face moved closer. 'Help me, Tyler.' It was all he ever said, and his voice seemed to come from down a dark tunnel, from the other side of death, an echo of a voice, and his breath was as cold as the grave. 'Help me.'

He began to reach out to me, ghostly hands, yet they appeared as real as my own. I was terrified. Terrified that if he touched me, if I, for one moment, felt the cold touch of those icy fingers I'd be dragged further into this nightmare. Dragged perhaps into his time. His past. 'Help me, Tyler,' he said again.

I stumbled back, away from those fingers, from those hands. I lost my footing and fell back hard on to the floor.

And suddenly everything began to speed up again. Jazz was running to help me, really running, out of the dream, rushing towards me.

'Are you OK?' She bent down to me, concern all over her face.

My shaking hands pointed to the dark recess of the corridor. 'He was there.' My voice was shaking. 'You must have seen him.'

But Ben Kincaid wasn't standing in the shadows now. 'He was there, I swear. He said . . . "Help me, Tyler."' I looked at both of them. 'I shouted back at him. I screamed at him. You must have heard me shouting.'

And I knew from their faces that they hadn't. Aisha said, 'Tyler, we were right behind you, you were just running so fast, and you turned round and . . . you just fell.' She looked at Jazz and raised her eyebrow.

'He was there!' I screamed again now. I glanced again

to where Ben Kincaid had been standing, and there was my proof. The statue of St Teresa, gazing down at me. Her eyes open, watching me. Her hands still outstretched. 'Look, the statue's moved. Her eyes are always closed. Her hands are always locked together, you know that. Now look at her! Her eyes are open. She's not praying. The statues move. The statues always move!' I grabbed at Jazz's jacket, stared deep into her eyes. She had to see, believe me.

Jazz turned and looked up. A crowd had gathered and they all looked too.

'That's the way she always looks, Tyler,' Aisha said. Her voice was stiff with resentment, as if I was making a fool of her. 'They're only made of plaster. That means they can't move.'

And when I looked back too, she was right. St Teresa was standing as she had always stood, hands clasped, eyes closed in prayer.

I scrambled to my feet, threw off their hands trying to help me. 'No, she moved. I see them move all the time. The statues move.'

'This is a new one,' Aisha muttered. And I knew then, by mentioning the statues, that I had lost her too.

And I didn't care. Why should I? 'I've seen them

move from the beginning! From that very first day! The statues move. And Ben Kincaid *was* there.'

'Maybe Mac's right. Maybe you are making all this up, like you did in your last school,' Aisha said.

'But maybe you can't help it. It's not your fault. Maybe you do need help, Tyler.' This was Jazz, and I so didn't want Jazz to stop believing me.

'No . . . don't say that.'

'But we've been here all the time, and nothing's happened.' Jazz was trying to understand it, I could see that. 'We were watching you. We were right behind you, Tyler. There was no one there. You didn't talk to anyone. We would have seen you. Nothing happened. You just tripped.'

'So, you decided to make something happen.' Aisha's voice was cold.

'You just want to agree with your boyfriend!' What made me say that? I was losing the only friends I had here. I looked at Jazz. 'I don't understand how it happened. Ben Kincaid was there and the statue moved! He said, "Help me, Tyler." That's all he ever says. Help me, Tyler.'

Everyone was muttering about me, sniggering about me. All looking at me, all with that same look on their faces. The look that said I was weird, the crazy girl. I couldn't take it. I pushed them out of my way, so roughly they began to get annoyed at me.

'Hey, watch what you're doing!' someone shouted.

'No wonder you were chucked out of your last school.'

What was the use of having friends anyway? Even if they stayed by my side every instant. No matter what I did, I couldn't stop what was happening. I couldn't change it. Ben Kincaid could still get through. Still reach out to me through the mists of time.

I was so afraid. Afraid to be in the school, and afraid to leave it.

29

I don't know how I got through the rest of the afternoon. I had never felt so miserable. Jazz and Aisha didn't even try to talk to me. And when the bell rang at the end of the day, I hurried out of school and down the long drive, lined with elms. I could hear the other pupils whispering all around me, giggling as they went past me. I didn't want to see them or be near them. I turned away from them and headed for the lake. I would stay there, I thought, till they had all gone home. Then at least I would avoid all their snide comments.

I made my way to the little arched bridge. Darkness was already falling. I stood and gazed down into the murky depths of the water, and tried to make sense of all that was happening.

Help me, Tyler . . . It was all he ever asked of me, but how could I help him? And help him to do what? Pass to the other side? That was what Jazz thought. He needed help to pass on. I had tried prayer and that hadn't worked. He was still here. He still needed me to help him. But how was I supposed to do that?

The trees around the lake were hung with a mist that settled around the branches like dark grey cotton wool. It seemed to muffle the sound of the world. I could hear nothing, see nothing beyond the trees, and no one could see me.

Except Ben Kincaid. Was he watching me now? From the long windows in the school, perhaps? Or from somewhere in his dark past.

'I don't know how to help you,' I said aloud. It was a plea.

For how could I possibly help a long dead boy? A boy whose body had never been found . . .

Whose body had never been found . . .

Help me, Tyler.

Did it bother him so much that his body was lost somewhere, that he had had no proper burial?

And was that what was holding his spirit here on earth?

Was that possible?

A few weeks ago I would have dismissed it as

nonsense, but now, after everything that had happened . . .

But how could I find his body when all those years ago the police, the professionals, had been unable to find a trace of it?

They'd even dragged this lake.

I looked again down into those murky waters. They had dragged this lake, and found . . . nothing. Divers had been sent down into the depths and they had found . . . nothing.

The depths.

Out of the depths . . .

Out of the depths I have cried to Thee, O Lord, Lord, hear my voice.

Ben Kincaid's prayer?

It had to mean something. And if that lake hadn't already been dragged, I would have been sure I had found the answer.

Ben Kincaid's body would be down there.

But the lake *had* already been dragged.

My thoughts were racing in my head, so fast I couldn't keep up with them.

Because, I was thinking, wouldn't the lake be a perfect place to hide a body after . . . after it had been dragged?

Who would look for a body in a place that had already been searched?

And it seemed to me in that moment I knew the answer to everything.

He wanted me to find his body. He wanted to have a burial, so that his spirit could leave the earth.

I remembered his plea that dark night in my bedroom. *Help me, Tyler.*

The tumbler marking out the same words, again and again. *Help me, Tyler.*

Why had it taken me so long to figure it out?

De Profundis. The monks' ghostly prayer, another clue for me to follow. Out of the depths. They had been telling me to look here, in the lake, for Ben's body. To have it lifted . . . out of the depths.

Trying to help me, to help Ben, to make up for the terrible sin one of their brothers had committed.

Everything that had happened had been leading me here. To this lake. Ben Kincaid's body was down there in the depths of that murky water.

The only thing I didn't know was . . . how on earth was I going to get the police to drag this lake again?

30

I thought perhaps Jazz or Aisha might phone me that night. But no one did. And why should they? They had done their best to help me, and yet I still claimed something had happened, right in front of their eyes. Something they hadn't witnessed, something impossible. No wonder they really couldn't believe what I was telling them.

I hardly talked to anyone when I came home, and when Mum came up to tell me dinner was ready I almost asked if I could have it in my room.

'Something's happening at school, isn't it?' she said, sitting down beside me. 'Don't you think I don't know you're unhappy there. You look so pale, you're never smiling any more. Now tell me what's wrong.'

'I don't want to worry you, Mum.'

'I'm your mother. It's my job to worry.' She put her

arm round my shoulder. 'If you're really that unhappy at the school, I don't want you to stay there. I told your dad that.' Her eyes had filled up with tears. I didn't want to make my mum cry.

'Tell me what it is that bothers you. I really want to know.'

I shook my head. She'd have me in therapy if I told her. I was sure of it.

She sniffed back a tear. 'You thought you saw someone who was dead at your last school . . . is it something like that again?'

I remembered how she would walk out of the room whenever I mentioned it. How could I tell her it was happening again?

Yet, I didn't have to answer her. She saw the answer on my face.

'I thought it might be something like that.' She pulled me closer. 'I know I wasn't much of a help to you that time . . . But you have such an imagination, Tyler. Perhaps what is happening to you is just your imagination again?'

I pulled myself away from her. 'I knew you'd say that. It's what everybody says. Always the same thing. Well, if this is my imagination, I must be mad.'

She clutched at my hand. 'Tell me then. Tell me everything.'

'I thought I must be seeing things at first. But I'm not. Too much has happened, is still happening. A boy died in my school, long ago, and I keep seeing him. He was murdered. He keeps asking me to help him, and I don't know how.' I buried my face in her shoulder. 'I know, this sounds crazy. I'm sorry.'

I heard her sigh. She was going to tell me I was going mad, I just knew it. Why should she believe all this? But now that I had told her this much, I realised I might as well tell her the rest.

'And the statues . . . Mum, the statues in the school keep changing. One minute their eyes are closed then they're open, watching me. One minute their hands are locked in prayer, and the next . . . they seem to be point-ing . . . reaching out to me.' I buried my face in my hands. I really was going crazy. Saying it aloud, it sounded absurd.

At first I thought she sighed again. But this time it wasn't a sigh. It was more of a shocked gasp. I looked up at her. Mum was staring at me. 'Tell me about the statues,' she said.

'They're everywhere in the school. And they watch

me, they look at me, then they look away. Their fingers point at me, then when I look again, those same fingers are pointing somewhere else. But no one else sees it, only me. Am I going mad? Tell me if you think I'm going mad.'

She was quiet for a long time. 'There is another explanation . . .' She spoke slowly and softly. 'Perhaps you have a gift. Some people do . . . maybe you're one of them.'

I could hardly believe what she was saying. Was Mum going crazy too?

'What kind of gift?'

Mum closed her eyes, took a moment to answer me. 'A gift for contacting the dead.'

Now it was me who gasped. Mum didn't believe in things like that. She had always dismissed ghosts and witches and the occult as the daftest things she'd ever heard of. And I'd always thought she dismissed them because they scared her too. Now, here she was suggesting that I could contact the dead? Jazz saying it, I would have expected. But not my practical, sensible mum!

'What would make you think I have this gift, Mum?' Now I was the one who sounded as if I didn't believe *her*.

'The statues,' she said. 'You talking about the statues

157

. . . it's made me remember something. Something that happened a long time ago, to my mother. I think she had a gift and didn't realise it. Or was scared to talk about it. I think perhaps you might have the same gift, Tyler.'

'My gran . . . had the gift . . . ?' My gran had been like Mum, down-to-earth, not given to wild fancies. She was dead now. I still missed her.

'I'm going to tell you a story, a true story, about your gran,' Mum went on. 'And it's because Gran was such a down-to-earth person, I know you're going to believe it. It's the reason I believe it.'

31

'You remember I had a brother?' Mum asked me. She was fingering her chain as if she was nervous.

I nodded. 'He died, didn't he? He was only weeks old?'

She never talked about this brother, Joseph, who had been born ten years before her. 'He was the first boy born into the family. Everyone loved him. It was all girls in our family till he came along. The golden boy, they all called him.'

She paused for a moment. I said nothing.

'Your gran was living with your grandad's mother when he came along. And your great-grandmother was a really holy woman. She was Catholic. She had statues all round the house . . . and holy pictures. On every wall. One of them was above the bed where your gran and grandad slept. A picture of Jesus.'

I felt the room grow cold.

Mum spoke as if she was in a dream. 'Your gran said she'd never really looked closely at the picture before, not until after little Joseph was born. She would be lying in bed, with the baby in the crib by her side, and she'd look up at that picture . . . and He'd be looking down on her, very gently, and holding out His hands to her. And she'd shiver and turn away from Him, because it looked to her as if He was saying, "You can only have him for a little while. But I want him back."'

'She should have told my great-granny to take the picture out of the room,' I said.

'She couldn't do that. Your gran was only a young girl then. She didn't want to offend her mother-in-law. She thought she'd hurt her feelings. And anyway, you know your gran, she was sure she was just being silly. When you've just had a baby, you are terrified something's going to happen to them. You get up in the middle of the night, just to make sure your baby's still breathing. I think all new mothers do that.' She smiled. 'So . . . she decided it was her imagination. She'd just had a baby, her emotions were all over the place.'

'But in the end, her baby did die,' I said softly. And though I had never seen my great-grandmother's old house, I could picture it. I was back there in that room, where my gran had slept. I could see the bed, the lamp, the crib, the picture above the bed, everything. I could feel the fear she must have felt too.

'Joseph was rushed to hospital one night, and . . . after a few days . . . he died. The family were devastated. Your gran was so heartbroken. Then, one night after the funeral she was lying in bed and she looked up at the picture again . . . and Jesus wasn't looking down at her any more. His eyes were turned to heaven, and His hands were held up, as if He was offering up something very precious. That's the way your gran described it to me. As if He was offering up something very precious.'

Mum squeezed my hand. 'I've seen that picture, and that is exactly what it's like. Yet, Gran swore those nights when she lay in bed with her baby that's not what she saw. The picture changed.'

'Didn't she ask? Did she tell anyone?'

'She told your grandad, but he said the picture had always looked like that. It was only her imagination. And she couldn't bear to tell anyone else. Maybe I was the only other person she told, years later. It was only a few weeks before she died. I think other things were happening to her then and she thought she was going crazy too. I saw the expression on her face, whenever I would go and visit her, and it was just like yours, Tyler. She kept going on about that picture, and I think now she was trying to talk to me about those other things . . . And I didn't listen to her . . . I couldn't listen to her, the way I couldn't listen to you. It always terrified me. Now I think perhaps your gran had some kind of gift, and she's passed that gift on to you.'

I thought about my gran. Had she been as terrified as me, with no one to confide in? I pulled my hand away from Mum's. 'You didn't listen to her! You didn't listen to me! How could you do that, Mum? You should have told me about this. I thought I was going mad.'

Maybe Gran had thought that too. Alone. Sure madness was creeping up on her.

Mum pushed her fist against her mouth. 'It makes me so afraid, Tyler. You said you saw someone who was dead . . . and your gran tried to tell me that too. Someone was in the house with her . . . someone dead . . . and I thought . . . she's just old, she's imagining things . . . I wouldn't believe her.' Her eyes were filled with tears. 'I was scared to believe her.'

'But when I told you about Miss Baxter, why didn't you tell me then.'

She sniffed back a tear. 'Because you were always one to tell stories, Tyler. When you were little you had an invisible friend, came everywhere with you. When we would go on holiday, you'd tell people we were on the run from the law. Always making up stories. Why should I have thought this was anything different?'

'You should have told me about Gran!' I snapped at her, and a second later, clutched her hand again. 'I'm sorry, Mum.'

Maybe she'd been right not to tell me, I thought. She would never do anything to deliberately hurt me. 'So you think the same thing might be happening to me?'

'If it could happen to someone as down-to-earth as your gran, why not you?'

'So . . . what does it mean, Mum?'

Mum put her arm around me. 'Gran said the picture was trying to let her know Joseph was only there for a short time. He belonged in heaven. Maybe the statues are trying to tell you something too.'

'Maybe that Ben Kincaid belongs in heaven too, if I can help him . . .'

Mum squeezed my hand. 'I don't know, Tyler . . . but you're not going crazy. And if you want, we'll start looking for another school for you. OK?'

I felt so much better when Mum left the room. I even agreed to have dinner downstairs. I wasn't going mad. There was maybe something in me that had been passed from my grandmother.

The statues were all a part of it, trying to tell me to help Ben Kincaid. And I thought, *I know how to do that now. If I can help find his body. He will be able to move on.*

All the talk round the table at dinner was about the girl who'd gone missing. Debbie Lawson. Her picture was on the front page of all the papers. And on the teatime news there had been a press conference and a heartbreaking plea from her mum and dad asking her to get in touch. They were devastated. Her mother looked as if she hadn't slept for weeks.

Mum was taking it badly. 'I couldn't bear it if one of you went missing.'

'They don't think she's missing any more,' Dad said. 'They think she's dead. That she was picked up here and killed here. They've started searching everywhere for her body now.'

Time stood still. As if everyone in the room went into freeze-frame.

They were searching for a body.

And all at once I knew exactly how I could get the police to drag the lake.

32

'You're telling me you saw something in the lake outside your school?' The big policeman seemed to tower above me. It took all my courage to look him straight in the eye. But I had to make him believe me. Yet, looking up at him made me feel dizzy – so I looked straight back down to the floor of the police station.

'Yes, sir. This morning. I was standing on the wee bridge over the lake . . . and I saw –'

'You saw . . . what . . . ?' His voice was a growl.

I swallowed. I'd already told him twice, now he had called some kind of plain-clothes policeman into the office with us and I had to repeat it again.

I had worked out carefully what I was going to say. I didn't want to be too specific. Didn't want to say I saw Debbie Lawson's body. But only hint that I might have. That would be enough, surely. Hadn't Dad said they had to follow up every lead, no matter how tenuous? They wouldn't take any chances. They were dragging the river for her. They were digging up waste ground. They were looking everywhere.

I went on, my voice trembling. 'Something under the water. I thought it was a doll, one of those inflatable dolls. She was lying face down, but she was dressed in pink . . . and I remembered about the girl . . . that Debbie girl. She was last seen dressed in pink, wasn't she?'

The policeman didn't answer me. I licked my lips and carried on quickly. 'And one minute she was there, and the next she was gone.'

'A body could be dragged down by reeds or ferns.' I saw rather than heard the plain-clothes man mutter this to the big policeman. He nodded. But a policewoman had stepped into the room now too. I hadn't even noticed her come in. When I glanced at her, she raised an eyebrow. Her eyes were ice. Harder to convince than her male colleagues.

'So why didn't you run into the school? Tell your headmaster?'

I had an answer, thought out, for that too. 'I thought I had to come to the police first . . . did I do something wrong?'

The policewoman recognised my tactics. Little inno-cent girl asking big man if she had done the right thing. I couldn't help but glance at her and her disapproving glare again.

The policeman growled. 'You did the right thing, lassie . . . but are you sure of what you saw?'

And I shook my head. I wasn't going to be too sure. I wanted to appear like some young girl who thought she genuinely might have seen something . . . not like some crazy teenager who made up stories.

'Maybe I was wrong? Maybe it *was* just a doll.' And I knew, by the look that passed between them, that they would take no chances.

Everything happened really fast after that. Phone calls were made, more people came to interview me. And finally they took me back to the lake in a police car, so I could point out where I had seen that . . . 'something'.

It was just then that Mr Hyslop came rushing across the drive. Someone must have gone in to inform him of what was happening. He looked furious. He stopped next to the big policeman with the gruff voice. His arms were waving about as if they'd been caught in a high wind. His face was beetroot red with anger. I'd never seen him so animated. Snatches of what he was saying drifted my way in the wind.

'. . . can't believe a word she says . . .'

'. . . always making up stories . . .'

'. . . been in trouble since she started in this school . . .'

I held my breath as the policeman stormed towards me with Mr Hyslop galloping in front of him.

'Tyler Lawless, what have you been trying to pull here!' Mr Hyslop yelled at me.

I felt my knees begin to buckle then. But I had to stay strong. I looked steadily at the policeman. 'Sir, I did see something in the lake. I don't know what it was . . .' I let the words trail away.

'You better not be making all this up, girl.' The big policeman looked at me in a different way now. I knew that look so well.

'I'm not, sir . . . I promise . . . Something was in the lake . . . I don't know what it was.'

The headmaster tutted. 'A complete waste of tax-payers' money. I can't believe you're dragging this lake on her say-so!' he muttered.

It was too late to stop anything now anyway. An underwater search unit had arrived, and when I glanced up at the old school there were faces at every window, vague, ill-defined faces, all eager to watch the excitement.

And I wondered, was Ben Kincaid's face somewhere up there? Was he at one of those windows, watching?

I was ordered into school, and I was informed by an increasingly angry Mr Hyslop that my parents would be sent for. I stepped into my class and I knew from all their faces that none of them believed what I had seen. Even Jazz looked fed up with me.

'You're making it worse for yourself, Tyler,' she whispered during one of the lessons. 'First Ben Kincaid and now Debbie Lawson? Oh, Tyler.'

She was sick of me. They were all sick of me. But they'd know soon enough. When Ben Kincaid's body was dragged up from the depths, they would know I wasn't lying. His body . . . or would it be his skeletal remains after all this time? It didn't matter; there would be ways they could identify him. They would find him and then everyone would know I was right.

We all watched, all that day, cramming round windows as we moved between classes.

Divers, all in black, slid into the water like seals. Time and time again I saw them, and every moment when their heads broke the surface, I held my breath waiting for them to call out they'd found it.

All day they searched, till the winter dusk began to settle on the afternoon.

But they found nothing.

An old rusty trolley.

A pram.

A bag full of dead kittens.

But nothing else.

Nothing.

'But I did see something,' I kept saying as I was dragged to the Rector's office. My parents were there, as well as the police. My mother looked as if she'd been crying.

Not one of them thought I had simply made a mistake. Not with my reputation.

'You could be charged with wasting police time, young lady.'

When the policeman said that, my mother gasped and covered her mouth with her hand as if she might cry out if she didn't.

'I did see something.' But my words were a mumble.

Mr Hyslop would never believe that. 'Of couse you didn't see anything. You're an attention-seeker, Tyler.'

He turned to the policeman. 'She's only been in the school a few weeks and the whole school recognises that. She's always making things up. Ghosts and strange noises and goodness knows what other lies.'

'They're not lies! I don't make things up!' I shouted at him. Only made myself look worse.

A stroppy teenager, that's what I was.

The policeman left with the warning that this matter would be put in the hands of the Procurator Fiscal, who would decide if there was a case to answer. I could be charged. I could end up in court. Mum began to cry again when he said that.

And it still wasn't over after the police left. The Rector wasn't finished with me.

'I'm afraid this is her last warning, Mr Lawless. I've heard all about her at her last school. She was disruptive there and she's a very disruptive pupil here too. And I can't have the likes of her in the school . . . unless she behaves herself.'

My last warning . . . again.

I tried to explain to Mum and Dad on the way home. But Dad wouldn't listen. He was way too angry with me. 'History repeating itself,' he said.

'You said I might have a gift,' I reminded Mum when

we were alone. 'You said maybe the statues were trying to tell me something.'

'You think they were trying to tell you to drag the lake for Debbie Lawson?' she snapped the words out. 'I should never have told you that story. It only gave you ideas. I just didn't want you to think you were going crazy. I don't want to hear any more about this, Tyler.'

If they were angry . . . I was even angrier. Angry and confused. I had done everything I could. So what was this Ben Kincaid after? Why was he haunting me? If his body wasn't in the lake, how the hell was I supposed to find out where it was?

I was in trouble with the police, in trouble at school. I had lost the few friends I had made here. All because of a dead boy who had had as bad a reputation as I now had.

I was finished with it, finished with everything.

Let Ben Kincaid do his worst. I was through with trying to help him.

33

Believe it or not the sun came out the next day. A weak, frosty sun, but the sun none the less. It should have cheered me, but nothing could.

I had to go back to school and face everyone. Mum and Dad wouldn't let me take a day off. Even though I begged them.

'It would be better if I stayed away. I'm on a last warning anyway,' I tried to tell them. 'I'll be so embarrassed.'

Dad had an answer for that one. '*You'll* be embarrassed! How embarrassed do you think we were yesterday! Well, you can face it today. You'll go back, my girl.' He sounded disgusted with me too. 'And I don't care if you witness the *Titanic* rising from that lake – ignore it – don't mention it to anyone – OK?'

So I went to school, dragging my feet. Knowing how

everyone was going to treat me when I got there. And I would know what they were all thinking of me. Jazz and Aisha and Adam and Mac. Mac especially. I didn't think I could take any more of his horrible comments. Or that disgusted stare of his.

There was a crowd of pupils at the gates at the end of the school drive, waiting for me. Somehow I knew they were waiting for me. They began to taunt me right away. 'Seen any dead bodies lately?'

I sidestepped past them, didn't even look their way, and almost tripped over a pair of legs that were sticking out from under a bush.

'Oh, look!' one of the girls said dramatically, pointing them out. 'A dead body. Who's going to report this?'

Another one called out to me, 'Oh, there's Tyler. Tyler, want to get the place searched for another dead body?'

I could hear the giggles from behind the bush and two of the boys appeared, each holding up a Hallowe'en dummy's leg.

I know they aren't real! I wanted to shout back at them. *I can tell the difference!*

It was the same all the way up the drive. Pupils

giggling, or pointing, or just staring at me. I'd have rather they turned their backs on me. Pretended I wasn't there.

Jazz and Aisha were standing at the entrance. At first I thought they were going to make a fool of me too. I did them an injustice. Jazz slipped her arm in mine. 'We thought you might need a bit of support today,' she said.

I felt my eyes fill with tears. Aisha took my other arm. 'Oh, don't cry on us now. Walk tall. Head high.'

So I did. Not so afraid with them beside me.

'I have to tell you about yesterday,' I started to say. I wanted to explain to them, but Aisha shushed me.

'Look, Tyler. Whatever made you do what you did yesterday is your business. Jazz and me decided we're not going to talk about that, OK?'

They weren't going to believe me, probably did think I was a bit mad. But even so, they were going to be there to support me. I felt like crying again.

Mr O'Hara glared at me as soon as I stepped into the classroom. After that, I could have been invisible. His eyes scanned the rows of desks but skimmed over me completely, as if I wasn't there. In fact, apart from the few who sniggered at me as I walked past them, the whole school ignored me.

All except Mac. At breaktime in the cafe, he banged into a seat across from me. 'What is it with you, always making a fool of yourself? Bodies in the lake! Getting the cops to drag it! Come on, get real. You're such an embarrassment.'

He went on so much Jazz told him to shut up.

'Why can't you just let her be, Mac?' Adam said.

And Callum agreed with him. 'What's it to you anyway? Why does it annoy you so much?'

'I think maybe you fancy Tyler. Maybe that's your problem.' It was Aisha who said it, taking me completely by surprise. Wasn't she the one who fancied Mac?

Mac jumped to his feet as if he'd been lifted by an unseen hand. 'Her! Tyler blinking Lawless!' He snapped my name out. 'You've got to be joking. She's the last one I'd ever fancy.'

And he stormed out of the cafe.

That almost made me cry again. Because in that moment . . . I knew I liked Mac. I liked his dark chocolate eyes, and his white teeth, and the way his hair hung over his forehead, and the way he had of swaggering when he walked. Oh no, it was me who fancied Mac!

And I had burned my boats with him too. He hated me.

I would have left at lunchtime, if it hadn't been for Jazz and Aisha. But nothing happened I couldn't handle because they were beside me, and the sun grew strong, and filled the long corridors with spears of yellow light.

But it didn't last.

It was between classes. The corridors were filled with herds of pupils stampeding to the next class.

And there he was again, standing amongst them, solid as they were. Ben Kincaid, staring at me.

I turned to Jazz and Aisha, right beside me, and it seemed they were in a different time. Moving slower than I was, and slower still, until they stopped, everyone stopped. As if time had been frozen.

I looked back at Ben Kincaid. His eyes were still watching me, but he began to back along the corridor. He wanted me to follow him. He beckoned me to follow him. Holding out his hands, calling me to him. 'Help me, Tyler.'

I didn't understand what was happening, but I wasn't going to let it go. Not this time. I was going wherever he led me.

34

The school was silent, every pupil still as death, moving yet not moving. As if they were the ghosts, not Ben Kincaid. I brushed past them, my eyes never leaving the boy I was following. He turned back to me at the end of the long corridor and his face was pale and there were shadows under his eyes. But he was as real as I was. How could he be a ghost? He was real. Or I was mad. I turned back for a split second to look at Jazz, held by some kind of magic.

When I turned back, he was gone. In the blink of an eye, he had vanished. The corridor led off in three directions, to the right, to the left, and straight ahead, up a short flight of steps. I hadn't seen which way he'd taken. There was no sign of him. No sound of him. Yet, I knew this time I couldn't let him go. I had to confront him. I had to exorcise Ben Kincaid. This had to be over.

I stood at the crossroads at the end of the corridor looking from one way to another. I felt like crying again.

And then something made me look up at the statue in the corner. She stood on her plinth, with a kindly smile on her face, roses at her feet and her alabaster hand outstretched. A saint who always had her fingers clasped in prayer, I was sure of it, with rosaries wound round her closed hands. Now the beads hung from her outstretched fingers. As if she was pointing down the corridor to the left, as if she was telling me, 'Go that way.'

The kindly face, the pointing fingers. The eyes watching me. The statues were always pointing, or looking a certain way. I remembered Mum's story about my gran. And the picture that had been trying to tell her something.

Was that what they had been doing all along, since I came here? Those statues that had so frightened me? Always helping me, always trying to show me the way. Never trying to make me afraid? Wanting me to help Ben Kincaid too?

I began to run, and as I ran I looked at each statue I passed. Each one pointed the way for me, first this way, then that, as I twisted and turned round corners, up staircases, while pupils barely moved around me. All the statues were telling me where to go, all sending me after Ben Kincaid. I didn't yet understand why. I only knew I had to follow where they led.

I was at the far end of the school now. The corridors were almost empty here. There were no classrooms. The only sound I could hear was the tap of my own footsteps. I had lost sight of Ben Kincaid, but I knew this time I wasn't going to lose him. The statues wanted me to find him. They'd always wanted me to find him. So that I could help him. They wanted to help him too. I knew that now as sure as I knew anything.

I stopped running. And looked behind me. The corridor stretched down into blackness, into the shadowy gloom. It was silent, empty.

The sky grew dark. I could see through the high windows the black, ominous clouds racing past. It was as if night had fallen fast.

I was alone here. My heart beat wildly. My mouth was dry as dust. Everything was strange, weird.

And now I was afraid. Afraid of the darkness all around me. Something was changing and I didn't know what.

Yet, I couldn't go back. Didn't know how, and anyway, didn't dare go back into that gloom. I could only go on. I had no choice.

There was another statue ahead of me. His eyes were turned towards me, watching me. I imagined they were alive. All the statues were alive. I imagined they could step from their plinths at any moment and walk beside me. I looked at his hands. And they were pointing down towards the chapel.

I had known it was here I was headed, here I was being led. The inevitable place to finish the story. Ben Kincaid was murdered there. I knew then that's where I would find him.

I began to run towards it.

35

The chapel door lay closed before me. But even as I ran towards it, the door swung open. As if it had been waiting for me. As if the chapel was waiting for me.

Expecting me.

I stepped warily inside. The chapel had been dark and silent when I'd come with Jazz and Aisha. Never used since Ben Kincaid's murder. A sacrilege had been committed here. I'd wondered why it hadn't been destroyed, if the memory of that murder had been so appalling.

Yet, here, now, the chapel had come alive. Candles were flickering around the statues, and there were more statues now too, not just St Anthony. There were statues in every alcove, on every altar. And every altar was draped with a crisp white cloth, trimmed with gold. There were fresh flowers in every vase and the air was filled with their scent, and with a hint of incense.

And still dominating it all, in the corner of the chapel, St Anthony. He carried the baby Jesus in his arms. I moved towards him, waiting for him to guide me, by a look, by a gesture. But nothing happened. He stayed still.

Why had I been brought here?

I looked again at St Anthony. He was the patron saint of lost things . . . and I clasped my hands over my mouth as I realised the truth.

The finder of lost things!

Standing high on his plinth.

My mind went back to the day we had all tumbled against another statue, and I had seen inside the plinth. And it had been hollow. Hadn't I seen how hollow the plinths were?

A space large enough for a body, for Ben Kincaid's body.

And it seemed to me in that split second I understood everything. Why I had been led here, to the chapel.

Out of the depths.

Not deep in the lake at all.

But in the depths of St Anthony's plinth.

I thought back to the night of the murder. The story

I'd read on a website. Father Michael desperately trying to think of where he could hide Ben's body. He only had moments to cover his terrible deed, and he saw the statue. Could he have moved it by himself? Lifted Ben's body, dropped it inside? He looked like a big, powerful man in the photo I had seen. It would be difficult, but not impossible.

And his mind was so taken up with hiding the body, that he'd forgotten to hide the other thing that could convict him . . . the knife with Ben's blood, and his fingerprints all over it. Perhaps he'd been disturbed, had heard someone coming, and had snatched up the knife slipped it in his pocket, and he had run.

I took a step back. My mind was racing. Surely this was the truth at last.

Ben Kincaid's body had been hidden in this chapel all along.

Could I move the statue myself? Impossible! Did I have the nerve to push it over? See Ben's bones tumble out on to the chapel floor? Did I even have the strength to push it over, smash it on the cold stone floor, see it fragment into tiny pieces? St Anthony? Or would that be a sacrilege too?

And did I have any other choice? No one would ever

listen to me again, not after yesterday. How could I convince anyone that Ben's body was there?

At that second, I heard the chapel door slam open, and I turned sharply.

Couldn't believe what I was seeing. Couldn't be happening!

Ben Kincaid came rushing in.

But not the Ben Kincaid I had seen with the pale face and the dark shadowed eyes.

No, this Ben Kincaid was bursting with life. And with something else. With fear. No, more than fear. Terror. I could see it in his wild eyes. There was sweat dripping from his brow.

He looked around the chapel, as if he was searching for somewhere to hide. Then he glanced back at the door. There was no silence now. I could hear footsteps pounding down the corridor towards the chapel, angry footsteps. Then Ben's terrified eyes turned to me. And I knew he could see me.

'Help me, Tyler,' he pleaded. 'Help me!'

Then he was past me, searching desperately for a hiding place.

'How can I help you?' I called to him, ran after him.

I even reached out to him, but my hands passed through his body and I stumbled back, terrified. He turned back for a second and his glance passed through me too. He couldn't see me. I seemed to have disappeared for him now.

He cowered at the foot of St Anthony's statue. I could hear those angry footsteps hurrying ever closer, and I saw the terror in Ben Kincaid's face . . . and I knew then what I was about to witness.

The murder of Ben Kincaid.

My heart drummed in my chest. I was as terrified as Ben now. I didn't want to watch this. Didn't want to be here. My eyes, like Ben's, were fixed on the chapel door. And the sound of those footsteps coming closer.

Any second now Father Michael would burst through, and I was afraid. I wanted to run, but there was no escape. Not for me. Not for Ben Kincaid.

The footsteps stopped. The door flew open with such force it crashed against a pew, sent it flying backwards to the floor. And Ben Kincaid's murderer came rushing in.

But it wasn't Father Michael.

It was Mr Hyslop.

36

It was the Rector. Mr Hyslop. Younger, as I'd seen him in the photograph outside his office, but unmistakable. His eyes were wild, mad eyes. He held the long, sharp knife in his trembling right hand, held it ready to strike.

He looked around, searching the gloomy chapel for Ben. 'You can't hide from me, Ben Kincaid.' There was madness even in his voice. It shook with fury. I moved further against the wall, as if he might see me too. But his gaze passed over me, unseeing. His anger terrified me.

The Rector had murdered Ben Kincaid. The truth of it amazed me and yet all at once it seemed so logical. Why shouldn't it be him? The teacher who had stayed in the school, rising to Rector. In control. Not allowing the chapel to be pulled down, keeping St Anthony there, isolated and alone, because that way the statue wouldn't be moved.

The statue that hid his secret.

The statue that hid his guilt.

And he'd let Father Michael take the blame? Why? How could anyone be so evil?

There was a sound: Ben stumbling back, trying to squeeze himself further behind the statue. Mr Hyslop caught sight of him then.

'There you are! There you are!' he screamed at him. He lifted the knife high. It was like a spear of silver caught in the candlelight.

Ben pushed himself far into the corner, but he had chosen a place with no escape. There was nowhere left for him to run. He was cornered, like a rat.

'Please!' he pleaded, his voice shaking with fear. But the Rector had no mercy in him. Madness has no mercy. He ran at Ben. In a second he would plunge that knife into him . . . Ben Kincaid was about to die, again.

NO!

Couldn't let that happen. Not again!

Some instinct took over. I didn't even know what I was doing. I ran from my hiding place, screaming, yelling, even though I knew I could do nothing to stop them, even though I knew they couldn't see me, still I ran between them, held up my arms and screamed out, 'Stop it! Stop it! Stop it!'

And the Rector fell back. His eyes flared in terror, and the knife dropped with an echoing clatter on to the chapel floor.

He could see me.

He crossed his arms in front of him, as if he was protecting himself from me. 'Who are you?' His voice trembled with terror. 'Who are you?' And then he crumpled to the ground. His eyes never left me. Not once.

I turned to Ben. He was still crouched behind the statues, watching me too. Tears of relief streamed down his face. 'I knew you would help me. I knew it . . . Thank you, Tyler, thank you . . .'

I was mixed up and afraid, and couldn't understand anything. I wanted to ask him what was happening, but he was on his feet, and running past me. Out of the chapel. I tried to grab him, wanted some kind of explanation, but once again, my hands touched only air. I wanted to scream out. Wanted someone to explain what was happening to me. But Ben was gone. Escaping while he could, afraid perhaps that the Rector would, even now, leap to his feet, snatch up the knife. Come after him again.

But there was no real fear of that happening. Not now. The Rector lay at the feet of St Anthony, whimpering. His whole body was shaking. He still looked at me, yet through me, terror never leaving his eyes. And in that second I realised the truth. That to him, I was the ghost.

I was the ghost.

He held out his hands towards me, spreading his fingers wide, as if he was shielding himself from me. As if I was some evil spirit he was desperate to ward off. 'Who are you?' he said again.

I could only stand and watch while he lay there, terrified, his eyes never leaving me. Was it seconds later or minutes? Time was nothing now. Another figure burst into the chapel.

And this time it *was* Father Michael.

He hurried across to the Rector, bent to him, took his hands in his own. His words were soft. 'What has happened here?'

The Rector's answer came in a sob. 'Father Michael . . . I almost killed him. I wanted to kill him. He had broken into the school. I found him stealing. You should have heard the way he taunted me. The way he always taunts me. I couldn't take it any more. I lost my mind. I wanted to kill him.'

'But you didn't kill him,' Father Michael said. 'In that final moment, you couldn't do it. You're not a killer, Robert.'

The Rector looked up once again at me. He raised a wavering hand. 'She stopped me, Father. I *would* have killed him, if it hadn't been for her. She saved both of us.'

Father Michael looked up then. How could I ever have thought his blue eyes were sinister? They were full of kindness and concern. But his gaze looked beyond me, or through me. And to him I was invisible.

'Who?' he asked.

'She's there, I tell you. Right in front of you . . .' The Rector's voice grew hysterical. His fingers clutched at Father Michael's robes. 'You must see her!'

Yet, when the Rector looked back I saw that I was gone for him now too. No longer there.

'Maybe,' Father Michael said softly, 'she was your guardian angel.'

He helped Mr Hyslop to his feet. 'No harm's been done here. I'll help you. You need to get away from this school for a while. We'll help Ben too.'

I stood unseen, watching them. Father Michael picked up the knife, slipped it into his pocket. Was that what had happened before? It seemed clear to me now. The Rector had killed Ben, hidden his body. The Rector was strong enough to do that. He'd been a mountain climber, an athlete. And when Father Michael arrived, the Rector had confessed to him, I bet he had. Mr Hyslop had confessed his crime, and so Father Michael had no choice but never to tell, to carry that confession to his own grave. And perhaps on that night long ago, he had also picked up the bloodstained knife, putting his own fingerprints all over it.

But what had happened here now? Had I really changed anything?

I watched as the Rector and Father Michael seemed to dissolve like smoke into the shadows of the chapel.

I was alone.

37

I was terrified to leave the chapel. Afraid of what I'd find out there. I looked up through the windows. The clouds seemed to be standing still, as if time itself had stopped. And then the sky changed, the moon disappeared, it grew light again, then dark. The clouds began to spin across the sky. The world was spinning out of control. It was as if I was on a rollercoaster. I stumbled against one of the pews, clutched at it to steady myself, and still the world spun. Faster and faster, I dared not look. I tried to move my hands to cover my eyes. I ordered them to move but they would not obey me. I was sure any second the sky would fall, the moon, the sun would come crashing down on me.

At last my hands moved. I folded my arms across my eyes and with nothing to hold on to I fell back against a pew and cracked my head. Did I black out? For a second

I thought I had, and then I heard the chapel door bang open. I screamed. I wasn't alone any more.

'Tyler, what on earth are you doing in here?'

It was Jazz. Could it really be Jazz? I peered over my elbow. 'Is that you?'

She stepped towards me nonchalantly. It was Jazz. Flesh and blood and pierced eyebrow and all.

'Are you OK?' She rubbed at my head. 'Did you trip up?'

I jumped to my feet. 'Oh, Jazz, something terrible happened in here.'

'Something's happened all right. We are going to get into so much bother. We're late for the next lesson.'

And Aisha was there too, holding open the door. She was trying hard not to smile. 'We've been hunting for you. What are you doing in here?'

I was dying to tell someone, to tell *them*. 'I stopped the murder. I don't know what it means, but I stopped the murder. I saw it all happening again in here, just moments ago.' Or . . . had it been thirty years ago? I was so confused.

Jazz glanced back at Aisha, then at me. What she said next stunned me.

'What murder?' she asked me.

I was puzzled. 'You know what murder. Ben Kincaid's murder. And it wasn't Father Michael who did it at all. It was the Rector, Mr Hyslop.'

Jazz stopped in her tracks. Pulled at me. 'What are you talking about, Tyler? Ben Kincaid got murdered? Am I missing something here?'

Aisha pulled us on. 'It's one of Tyler's stories. Tell us on our way to class.'

'It's not one of my stories.' I had to make them understand. 'It really happened. What are you two talking about?'

'If you're writing a murder story,' Aisha said. 'You'll have to have a more convincing killer than Father Michael. Everybody loves him. He had a massive, and I mean MASSIVE, retirement party last year, didn't he, Jazz?'

Jazz nodded. Still eager for us to move on. We were running now, turning corners, hurrying down corridors.

'Father Michael died in prison.'

Aisha laughed. 'So that's the story. Well, if you're going to set a murder story in this school, you'd better change the names.'

Jazz laughed. 'Yeah, 'cause Mr Kincaid might be a bit

annoyed if you kill him off. He's getting married next year.'

My head was still spinning. 'Mr Kincaid.' I stopped dead.

'The teacher. Honestly, Tyler. Sometimes I think you've got a head full of cotton wool. Especially when you're writing a story.'

'And talking of Mr Kincaid, here he comes,' Aisha said. 'And he's going to kill us for not being in class. And there's a murder for you!'

I looked down the corridor, and there he was, striding towards me. I still recognised the boy in him, though he was a man now. The same mane of dark hair, but tinged with grey, the same dark eyes. Mr O'Hara was by his side; they were laughing. Still friends.

Ben Kincaid had lost that haunted look I had seen in him so often. His eyes were bright. He hadn't seen me yet.

It was Mr O'Hara who noticed us first. 'Right, you girls. I might have known it would be you three! What are you doing wandering about the corridors? Get to class. Right now!'

Aisha hurried on to the class. But Jazz pulled me towards her. 'It was Tyler, sir. She didn't feel well. Look, she's still dead pale.'

Mr O'Hara smiled. 'You three have always got an excuse.'

But I was sure I *was* pale as death. I couldn't take my eyes from Ben Kincaid, now a man. Only moments ago I had seen him as a terrified boy. He stopped in front of me. 'Are you feeling OK now, Tyler?'

Hearing his voice again, I felt like fainting, black spots dancing in front of my eyes. So close, so real. A grown man . . . when only minutes ago . . . I stumbled against him, and the books he was carrying tumbled to the ground.

'You look as though you've seen a ghost,' he said.

I have, I wanted to tell him, *and the ghost was you*. Or was it me? Was I the ghost?

But I didn't need to tell him, because I was sure I saw in his eyes that he knew, knew everything. Remembered me.

I bent to help him pick up the books. Handed them to him. 'Thank you, Tyler,' he said. His voice so soft the others couldn't hear him. Only me. 'Thank you.'

Then he moved off with Mr O'Hara. I watched him. A man with a future and a past . . . Was that all thanks to me?

Jazz grabbed me again. 'Come on, you! I have something fantastic to tell you.'

If only she knew what I could tell her. 'What?' I asked.

'I know who it is Aisha fancies.'

'I thought we said it was Mac?'

Jazz looked at me as if I was mad. 'Mac . . . ? We would have to prize his eyes away from you first.'

Now I was completely mixed up. Mac? Liked me?

'It's Callum,' she said.

'Callum . . . ?' Why hadn't we even considered Callum? Yet, so often when Aisha couldn't come somewhere, neither could Callum! 'Of course,' I said. 'The night of the seance . . . neither of them could make it.'

Jazz let out a big sigh. 'Seance? What seance?'

The seance had never happened. Had never needed to happen. What else had changed?

We ran to our class, and as I ran I knew I was relieved it was Callum Aisha liked, because I had never wanted it to be Mac. We walked into the classroom and Mac looked up then, and he didn't glare at me, or look annoyed at me. Instead, he smiled with his warm . . . oh so warm brown eyes, and he winked.

And I laughed. I'd never felt so happy in my life,

because in that moment I realised I had changed everything. I wasn't on my last warning at the school. The
Procurator Fiscal wasn't going to charge me with wasting police time. I hadn't done any of the crazy things
that had made Mac hate me. I had never seen the statues
move. Never had the lake dragged. Because, thanks to
me, Ben Kincaid hadn't died . . .

And Mac liked me.

38

I learned more over the next few days. Got used to the fact I had changed everything. Ben Kincaid had indeed been a wild child, always in trouble, the bane of his poor, harassed mother. A boy everyone agreed was heading for a life in prison. Even the kindly but firm Father Michael's patience was stretched by his behaviour. He was the one everyone expected to snap. Yet, it was Mr Hyslop who had the nervous breakdown. A strong, athletic young man, he had always seemed able to handle Ben Kincaid's bad behaviour. But he had only been holding in a terrible anger, an anger that had burst to the surface the night Ben Kincaid broke into the school. No one actually knew what had happened that night. Mr Hyslop had been admitted to hospital, and a shaking Ben Kincaid had been questioned by the police but never charged. Father Michael had taken him in hand after that. It seemed that had been the making of Ben Kincaid. He had changed. If not into an ideal pupil, that was too much to hope for, at least into your typical teenage boy. Made up with his friend Gerry O'Hara, and been involved in all the high spirits and stupid pranks that most teenage boys get up to, but never after that did he cause any real trouble.

And so Father Michael had a long and happy career at St Anthony's College . . . and Ben's mother didn't die of a broken heart . . . and I didn't have the lake dragged, because I had never seen any ghosts or any moving statues.

And Debbie Lawson came home. She had seen her parents on television, heard about the police digging up waste ground, dragging rivers looking for her body, and her guilt had brought her home.

I did try to tell Jazz and Aisha all that had happened, and Jazz, crazy Jazz, had an explanation.

'Remember the day you arrived at the school, you took a tumble outside the Rector's office?'

And of course I remembered.

'You were unconscious. You were knocked out. You dreamed it all. You saw the statues in the school, the photos on the wall, and your imagination did the rest.

It's a great story . . . but, it isn't real, Tyler.'

And I wondered . . . was she right? Did I dream the whole thing? Or . . . is there another explanation?

My grandmother had the gift. Have I some kind of gift too?

And, what if it was true? And I really did change the past? It was such a strange experience. I'll never be able to explain it or understand why it happened.

But you know, all of it has made me think.

I changed the future by changing the past. And I began to remember . . .

'I saw my teacher in the queue at the supermarket last Christmas . . .' I can picture her now. Looking over everyone's heads as if she wanted me to see her, her eyes searching just for me.

But she was dead. She'd died in a tragic accident. An accident that should never have happened.

That should never have happened.

What if . . . What if I could change that too? What if that was what I was meant to do? What if that was why she'd come to me in the first place?

Do you think I'm silly thinking like this?

Or, do you think . . . I should try changing things again?

Loved *Out of The Depths*?

Then turn the page to find out about Cathy
MacPhail and her inspiration for this gripping story

Why I wrote *Out of The Depths*

I love where ideas come from – it's magic! I've taken ideas for books from almost everywhere, even from a sign on a wall, but this is the first time I've written a book based on just the first line.

Tynecastle High School in Edinburgh asked me to give them the first line for a short story competition. The first line is really important because it has to draw the reader into the story straight away. The line I came up with was this one.

'*I saw my teacher in the supermarket last Christmas. I was surprised to see her. She'd been dead for six months.*'

I thought it was a pretty good first line – it's intriguing, with lots of possibilities. Then I went back to the school after the competition and the pupils were all asking me whether I was going to write a book using this first line. Now that was a challenge I couldn't resist. I began to imagine that a girl comes into school one day and says she saw a teacher who had died the year before. Who would believe her? She'd be called a liar or they'd say she was going crazy. How would that make her feel?

Angry? Upset? Yes, both, but perhaps she'd also be determined to find out the truth. So the story began to grow.

When I get an idea for a story it's as if my brain is a magnet and it attracts other things I need to bring my story to life. I visited another school, an atmospheric old building with stone statues everywhere. The pupils thought their school would be the perfect background for a story and I thought they were right. I had my idea, I had my location and now all I needed was a name for my main character. I found it at another school I visited, where I met a bright-eyed girl who loved writing. As soon as she told me her name, I knew it was perfect for my story. Tyler Lawless was her name, and suddenly *Out of The Depths* was born.

At the beginning of *Out of The Depths*, Tyler has been practically expelled from her last school because of her story about seeing the dead teacher. She arrives at St. Anthony's College and finds herself drawn into a different mystery. I thought I had known how *Out of The Depths* ended the whole time I was writing it, and then I realised that if I'd known the ending, maybe all my readers would know too. So, I decided that there had to be something else, another twist to the story, and it was then that Tyler Lawless acquired a very special gift. A gift that even I, the writer, hadn't known she had. A gift that she could use over and over again.

There are lots of little twists to the plot in *Out of The Depths*, things that lead the reader to question what they think is really happening – one of them is in the title. And there is a reason I named the school St. Anthony's College . . . I love concealing mysteries within mysteries. But if you think you're going to unravel the mystery of the dead teacher in this book, think again. For that, you will have to keep a close eye on forthcoming books featuring Tyler Lawless.

Meet Cathy MacPhail

Cathy MacPhail was born and brought up in Greenock, Scotland, where she still lives. Before becoming a children's author, she wrote short stories for magazines and comedy programmes for radio. Cathy was inspired to write her first children's book after her daughter was bullied at school.

Cathy writes spooky thrillers for younger readers as well as teen novels. She has won the Royal Mail Book Award twice, along with lots of other awards. She loves to give her readers a 'rattling good read' and has been called the Scottish Jacqueline Wilson.

One of Cathy's greatest fears would be to meet another version of herself, similar to the young girl in her bestselling novel *Another Me*. She is a big fan of *Doctor Who* and would love to write a scary monster episode for the series.

Cathy loves to hear from her fans, so visit **www. cathymacphail.com** and email her your thoughts.

Q&A with Cathy MacPhail

What are your favourite things to do when you're not writing?

When I'm not writing, I'm usually reading or visiting family – I love spending time with my children, turning up on their doorsteps when they least expect me! I enjoy going on cruises too because it's the perfect way for me to visit new places. Like most people, I also love going to the cinema. I always have done.

What are your favourite films?

Oh, there are so many films I love. *It's a Wonderful Life* is one of them. The hero is an ordinary man with just a few problems that are getting him down. Then he is visited by an angel who shows him how life would have been if he had never been born and he realises that his life is worthwhile after all.

Another fantastic film is *The Searchers*. A story set in America in the mid nineteenth-century about a man's struggle to find his niece who has been kidnapped by the Sioux. It explores issues of racism that were common at the time.

But at the top of my list is *Some Like It Hot*. Two men

pretend to be female musicians to escape gangsters and one of them falls in love with Marilyn Monroe! It's so funny and it has the best last line of any film I've ever seen, 'Oh well, nobody's perfect.'

If you could be a character from a book, who would you be?

I have thought and thought about this because most books I've read have at least one wonderful character that I'd like to be, but I think Elizabeth Bennet has to be my first pick. She is so bright. Then there's Cathy from *Wuthering Heights*. I like her passionate nature, and we share a first name! Also, both of them are admired by fantastic men. When I'm really old, I want to be Miss Marple. I will go around annoying people and solving murders.

Have you ever seen a ghost?

I've not actually seen a ghost, but I'm sure I have felt the presence of one. I was at the Tyrone Guthrie Centre in Ireland, which I'd been told was haunted. I thought the haunted room was upstairs and so as I had a room on the ground floor, I assumed I was safe. Then I was woken in the night by something, or someone, sitting on my bed, moving closer. I was really scared. Finally I had the courage to leap from the bed and turn the light on. There was nothing in the room to be frightened of, but when I looked at my door the keys were swinging as if someone had just left the room. The keys kept swinging all night. I know this because my eyes never left them. In the morning, I learned there was no particular haunted room, but instead the ghost chose a different room to haunt every year. I used this incident as material for *Out of The Depths*.

Dying to know what Cathy eats for breakfast or what her favourite book is? Email your question to **childrensmarketing@bloomsbury.com**.
Five questions will be selected at random to be published in her next book, *Secret of the Shadows*.

Cathy's Choice

My Three Favourite Detective Stories

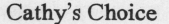 It was my son, David, who read *The Falcon's Malteser* first. He loved it so much he wrote to the Children's Film and Television Foundation to tell them they had to make it into a film. When they did, he took all the credit! Then, to his delight, he received a letter from the author, Anthony Horowitz. While on the set of the film, Anthony had heard about David's enthusiasm for the book and so invited him, and me, to London for the film premiere. As you can see, I have many happy memories of this book. It's exciting and funny, and it has some great characters. What more can you ask for in a good book!

How can anyone not love *Millions* by Frank Cottrell Boyce? It's heart-warming and tear-jerking, often all on the same page. It's the story of what happens when a bag stuffed with money drops from the sky and two boys find themselves very rich. Damian and Anthony are such lovely characters and their dialogue is perfect. *Millions* is one in a million – pure gold.

Sherlock Holmes is such a great character and an inspiration to many other detectives. There are so many wonderful Sherlock Holmes stories that I would be hard-pressed to pick a favourite.

If you loved *Out of The Depths*, dive into these books

COMING SOON

Seriously spooky stories, with punchy plots
and feisty characters, guaranteed to thrill
every reader

Catch up with Cathy at www.cathymacphail.com

Tyler Lawless returns with more nerve-tingling tales from the unlawfully dead

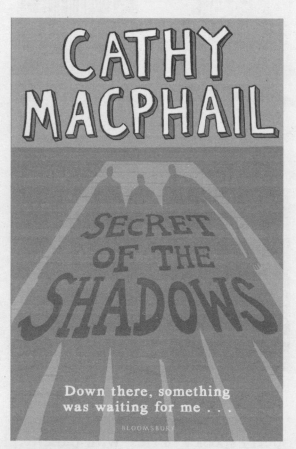

Spooking readers from March 2012